A CRUEL MADNESS

Colin Thubron is the author of several classic master-pieces of travel writing, including *Among the Russians*, *The Lost Heart of Asia* and *In Siberia*. His fiction titles include *Falling*, *Distance*, *Emperor*, *Turning Back the Sun* and most recently *To The Last City*.

ALSO BY COLIN THUBRON

Non-Fiction

Mirror to Damascus
The Hills of Adonis
Jerusalem
Journey into Cyprus
Behind the Wall
Among the Russians
The Lost Heart of Asia
In Siberia

Fiction

The God in the Mountain
Emperor
Falling
Turning Back the Sun
Distance
To the Last City

Colin Thubron

A Cruel Madness

VINTAGE

Published by Vintage 2004

11

Copyright © Colin Thubron 1984

Colin Thubron has asserted his right under the Copyright,
Designs and Patents Act, 1988 to be identified as the author
of this work

First published in Great Britain in 1984 by
William Heinemann

Vintage
Random House, 20 Vauxhall Bridge Road,
London SW1V 2SA

The Random House Group Limited Reg. No. 954009
www.randomhouse.co.uk

A CIP catalogue record for this book
is available from the British Library

ISBN 9780099437192

Penguin Random House is committed to a sustainable future for
our business, our readers and our planet. This book is made from
Forest Stewardship Council® certified paper.

Printed and bound in Great Britain by Clays Ltd, St Ives plc

For John, Virginia
and Llantina

"And most of all would I flee from the cruel madness of love –
The honey of poison-flowers and all the measureless ill."

Tennyson

One

It was built as a bedlam more than a century ago, and became a prison, then a lunatic asylum long after that. The older inmates still call the central block 'the madhouse', and sometimes, when the mist pours off the Black Mountains, you might think the whole institution a Gothic fantasy. The grey-red walls rise four storeys high to gables and slate roofs, and above them the twin chimneys of the laundry vents shoot up in polygonal cylinders, belching smoke as if this were Auschwitz, and banded in steel. All along the façade the pointed windows are meshed in iron. At night they turn into a bank of thinly-curtained lights, whose different colours resemble stained glass shining from the nave of some desanctified cathedral.

But in summer the enclosed gardens flower into a sombre beauty. There are handsome, isolated trees: cedars, yews and willows. Glass galleries circle the building's southern front, where the inmates sit as if ripening in the sun. A few pavilions scatter the lawns. From the highest wards you can glimpse a road beyond the outer walls, and a village in a dip of the hills. But that's all. The hospital is self-contained. It's like a factory devoted to nothing but its own upkeep; because hardly anybody ever comes out of it.

I came here as an occasional voluntary worker years ago. You get used to the place, of course, but sometimes even now I feel a pang of pathos or horror for it. Worst of all are its corridors, which are tiled in buff and green and look indestructible.

You can walk here for miles. The passageways are lit from above by canopies of clouded glass or by orbs of electric light which appear only to shed down dimness. You pass locked doors labelled 'pharmacy', 'culinary', 'mortuary', and occasionally glimpse constricted courtyards, just tarmac and rubbish, where black-lagged pipes wind from roof to roof. In winter suspended air convectors breathe down a heat which makes you dizzy. and loudspeakers in the passage angles relay soothing music.

The corridors resound with the shouts and mutterings of the patients, talking not to one another, but to voices from their past. They wander the labyrinth gesticulating and answering inaudible questions. Then it feels as if there's nothing here at all but memories, and even these may be of things that never happened. There's no real present here, and no future. There's only this past. Whisperings and laughter. They are mostly old now – if you can talk of *them* at all. Because nothing really lives in them except the long-dead. For most of them even fear, the last dignity, has faded. The past has left merely these husks and jabberings. With its grey cells and corridors, the whole place resembles a single magnified and shattered brain, in which each inmate is only a wandering memory-trace.

But much of the time the chronic patients don't strike you forcibly at all. You tend to forget they're there. Most of them are dressed in cast-off clothes: outsize shoes, old slouch caps and the striped ties of long defunct clubs. The women wear fashionless clothes of the fifties. They are frail, white-haired old ladies, for the most part, with brutally cropped hair. Some of the men are convulsed by tics or body-flailing or fevered interlacings of their hands; or their arms and legs have been set writhing by the long-term effects of Largactil. They trip or wobble or tiny-step down the corridors.

In the old days the community hall and social room would be overflowing; but television has changed that. Now most of the Chronics stay in their wards for days on end, except for visits to Occupational Therapy. They simply stare at the television, and smoke. Their wards have to be redecorated every

2

three years to cleanse them from a coat of nicotine. So the communal areas fall to a vagrant populace too restless to stay anywhere long. A few of them converse together, or engage in dual monologues which look like conversation. For a long time many of them make perfect sense, then one may ask suddenly "Why didn't you write to me before now?" or turn rigid and say: "It's cold here in Siberia."

Once a week I teach English to the Faraday ward, which is almost the only unit for short-term patients (although 'short-term' can mean over a year.) Compared to the rest of the hospital this ward is sharp with a sudden sanity and anguish. The Faraday men are all in acute stages of mental illness – mostly schizophrenics and psychopaths. They're heavily drugged, but perfectly coherent. That's typical of the severe Acutes. They are not insane like the Chronics, and they're mostly aware of their illness. A few are intelligent. Most are desperate to get out, and may simulate normality with great cunning; but others are so deeply withdrawn that they fight with the same cunning against leaving at all.

All the same, this work comes as a relief from teaching in the local prep school, because the Acutes are quite unpredictable. Their essays are introverted, of course, and may wander into incoherence; but one or two of them have written violently expressive poetry and short, perfectly lucid stories. A month ago I began an essay competition for the whole hospital, entitled 'The Most Important Time of my Life'. This kind of work can be useful to the unit psychiatrist as well as cathartic for the patients, and six or seven of the men in Faraday began writing in different parts of the ward: some in the television room, some in the dormitory, two in the kitchen.

It was while I was reading one of these essays by the light of a dormitory window, and sometimes staring absent-mindedly down into the gardens, that I was shaken by the sight of the woman walking along the path below. Even after she'd sat down on one of the benches, and only the back of her head was visible, I was certain I knew her. For a full five minutes I went on looking down. She didn't move. She was gazing in front of her where the mauve and yellow crocuses spread under the

3

trees. She must have been at least eighty yards away, but whenever she turned her head, however slightly, it brought a spasm of recognition.

For a minute or two I was bewildered as to why she was here. Then I realised: of course, she is a doctor. She must have a patient in one of the wards. Perhaps it was even somebody in Faraday – Sheldon, maybe, or Evans. I walked to the door, planning to go down, but stopped as I closed it behind me. I wasn't even surprised that after so many years she should still frighten me. But it was all rather pathetic, I suppose: this monkish schoolmaster, no longer young, dithering at the top of the stairs, afraid of a woman he hadn't seen for half his adult life. I was no longer even sure which of us should have forgiven the other. Or even precisely what there was to forgive. Except there was this resurrected ache; and a feeling that it was all immeasurably long ago, longer than its ten years, another incarnation.

In the end I went downstairs and let myself out by one of the side-doors. I half expected her to have gone. As I walked across the lawn I suddenly wondered what on earth I was going to say to her. I couldn't even envisage a proper greeting. I was disgusted to see that my hands were trembling. I thrust them into my pockets. When I emerged behind the yews only twenty yards from where she sat, she hadn't moved at all. She might have been made of stone. Her gaze wasn't fixed precisely on the crocuses, but on some other point farther away, on the field beyond perhaps, or on the distant wall, whose summit glinted with broken glass. I could see a part of her face clearly: the contour of a cheek-bone and the jaw-line. My shoulders started to shake. I had to slip back behind the trees to calm myself. But I couldn't stop this humiliating trembling. It's been ten years, I thought, and I'm still in this funk. I patted my hair forward and tried to slap colour into my cheeks, but felt them drain instantly. Then I had a second of imagining myself in her eyes, with my hair so much receded since I knew her and my complexion turned to a mouldy crumpet colour. I suddenly realised I must look completely middle-aged, although I'm only forty. What I expected from this meeting, I

4

don't know, but I even caught myself turning round to go back into the hospital. This cowardice slightly alarmed me. I lectured myself (in a way copied from my father). What are you afraid of? All there is here is a chance encounter with an old (thirty-eight now) girl friend, sitting on a rickety bench in an obsolete looney-bin. And you're shivering like the palsy.

"Sophia."

As I spoke, I was still standing by the yew trees, but she hadn't turned round. She went on gazing at somewhere beyond the crocuses. I came and stood in front of her.

"Sophia. Sophia, it's Daniel."

I was looking down on the smoothness of her hair, straight at the roots then tumbling into curls as I remembered; but it was dry, lustreless. She might not have heard me at all. Her eyes went on staring on a level with my waist. She hadn't answered, and she clearly didn't mean to. I thought: damn it, it's *I* who should be forgiving *her*.

I felt a sudden bitterness. "Sophia, it's been ten years. Won't you even look at me? *Look at me!*"

I crouched in front of her on a level with her eyes. I must have half forgotten the power of them, or else I'd under-estimated my weakness. They were not precisely angry, but fixed, burning. They gutted me, just as they always had. My breath was coming cold and fast. I wanted to stretch out a hand to her, but couldn't. And it was in her hands that I first noticed the change. They were folded on her knees, still slender; but where once the skin had stretched tight and delicate over the bones, it crumpled round the veins and tendons now, and was brown with liver spots. Even the flesh of her fingers was no longer firm, but hung between the joints in little translucent folds. I thought: I've kept her in my mind unchanged, but of course she's a decade older, like me.

But I think it was already dawning on me. When I looked back at her eyes they no longer seemed quite the same. I'd slightly shifted my stance, but she continued to gaze over my shoulder, as if I'd never been there. I realised then that they weren't seeing me at all, or anything. They were vacant,

5

undreaming. It was as if the person behind them had retreated far inside the skull, and had subtly abandoned them. If you didn't meet this stare head-on, they were dead.

I let out a sound between a sob and a groan. It startled me, as if it had been hers. But I was looking at the rest of her face now. Something had happened more profound and total than the crawl of lines about the eyes and forehead, or the dried lips or the spring of unplucked hair on her upper lip. It was more as if an inner luminosity had simply died, as if the body inside had given up. Even the shape of the face had changed; its weight had transferred downwards, where it created a new shapelessness about the jaw, and tiny pouches at the mouth's corners. The flesh around her chin looked vaguely misshapen and scarred. I suspected she'd had plastic surgery.

I stood up, a little to one side of her. She didn't move. For a full minute I watched her numbly, not knowing what my next feeling would be, simply observed her in quiet as I might have observed some flawed piece of furniture. She continued to sit erect, with her knees together and her hands folded on them. She appeared neat and composed, but her flowered dress, I realised now, had that indefinable look of jumble, and her shoes were heavier than she'd have chosen.

A tightness gathered at the base of my throat and stiffened and throbbed all through my neck. But I couldn't take my eyes from her and I couldn't weep. So I sat down beside her with one hand close to her, not touching, and for a while remained like this, feeling a temporary comfort, and following her gaze over the crocuses and into the field. And I slowly understood that in some part of me, secretly, I was glad to have found her like this, even the shell of her, because this was, in the end, the only state in which she would accept me.

She hadn't moved since I'd come. So still was she that her eye-blinks were faintly disturbing, as if a waxwork lived. Then I reached out and took one of her hands. She gave a start. She half turned to me, but stared only at my chest. The hand was dry and warm. She let it rest in mine.

I said: "Sophia. It's Daniel Pashley. Daniel. Do you remember Daniel?"

6

"Daniel," she said, so calmly that I thought it was the start of a sentence; but she let it hang there.

"Do you remember me?"

To my astonishment she said: "Yes."

"Do you?"

"Yes . . . remember you."

"Do you? At the school, Sunningrove. You remember that?"

"The school."

Now that I heard her voice again, its tones and inflexions returned to me one by one with peculiar painfulness. I had remembered her looks minutely, but I had somehow forgotten her sound. It was a low voice, musical, but thinner.

"You remember the school? An English teacher. Daniel Pashley. You came there."

"Where?"

I was kneading her hand as if to warm back memory through it. "Sunningrove. Try and remember. Daniel."

"Daniel." A trace of recognition in the sound, as if she were thinking about it.

"Look at me."

She turned her head, but gazed over my shoulder. She repeated: "Look at me." Her palms opened on her knees. "Transparent. See through me."

"What?"

"I'm glass."

"I can see you, Sophia."

"Now you see me, now you don't!"

Oh God. The tears were pouring down my face. For a minute more I sat beside her, but could think of nothing to say.

Suddenly she got to her feet. "She's gone shopping," she said. "Gone shopping . . . she'll be away an hour . . . maybe more . . . she never says . . ."

She began walking back over the lawn, her hand still in mine. Her long, springy step was unchanged from ten years. I went alongside, unable to stop her or alter her direction, as if she were a machine. But as we reached the side-door I was seized by panic. I had the idea she was going to vanish, just as

7

she seemed to have come. I stopped dead, still grasping her hand. "Which ward are you in, Sophia? Which ward?"

But she wrenched her hand away with a sharp cry. Her eyes were suddenly alive with resentment—it was the first time I felt she'd truly seen me. They made me wonder if she didn't know perfectly well who I was. She's schizophrenic, I thought; she's concealing her unbalance behind a screen of pure madness. That's what they do. But then I thought: that's just my wish, my longing.

The next moment she was climbing the stairs, oblivious of me. I followed her to see where she went. We arrived in the corridor which leads past the kitchens and Industrial Therapy to the women's wing. Once we had to flatten ourselves against the walls while two student nurses ran by with an empty stretcher trolley. She went with her old, confident step, until she reached the entrance to the female wards: an iron door pierced by a curtained panel. I touched her shoulder and said "Sophia, wait, wait just a moment", but she might not have felt or heard. She rapped against the panel, keeping her eyes averted from me. The curtain was pulled back by a charge nurse, and the door opened. I couldn't follow her.

As I heard her footsteps going away, I was overcome by an absurd desolation.

Two

I've been here half my life. I was here ten years ago, when I met Sophia. I arrived eleven years before that. And I still haven't gone.

It must be one of the most run-down preparatory schools in the country. Sunningrove: imagine a four-storey brick colossus louring above windswept playing-fields, an undersized swimming-pool and a few outbuildings set aside for inessentials (music, art.) The school colours are red and green, which is grotesquely right. Brick, grass. There's little else in sight. The only expression on the colossal red face is a dribble of black fire-escapes, running from roof to earth like disastrous worry-lines. The playing-fields slope away to woods, which are out-of-bounds and where a lake is sunk in a bed of rhododendrons, which flower for two weeks at the start of the summer term, then return to darkness. The lake's gloom is exacerbated by memory: before my time one of the school cooks drowned herself in it. The whole surface is glazed by a pale green scum, broken here and there by concentric rings, where something might have dropped in years ago. All around, the rhododendrons' bodies are gouged out by the dens and passageways of the boys, and gape like caves wherever they have been entered. Nobody obeys the out-of-bounds rule. Only when McQuitty wants to punish a boy, and can't find a specific excuse, he'll say *"You were seen in the woods."*

Three generations of McQuittys have run the place now. Their portraits adorn the dining-room much as the framed photographs of presidents watch over the offices of East European states. Their expressions are subsumed by a common, prestigious deadness, as if the headmastership immunised them from human frailty. They don't smile. They look down from another stratosphere on the long tables with their watery porridge or wafer-thin beef (every other Saturday) and prunes or rice-pudding (Tuesdays) as though they had nothing to do with it. But their hypocrisy is plain, because beneath the portrait of the youngest incumbent, James R. McQuitty M.A., sits the living flesh. The painted man is grave, scholastic even; his unindented cheeks and little greenish eyes might be construed – if not as benign (the portrait-painter has his integrity), then at least as harmlessly abstracted. But underneath this symbol sits the actual McQuitty, unconscious of incongruity. He is formidably gross. The hair is greying from his head in a russet dust, and the jowls slop and shudder over his collar. Seen from behind, the red bulge of his neck is as broad as the head above it. But he is only forty-seven. He emanates a kind of predatory unease, restless with something I don't know. He isn't married (the grotesque dynasty will die with him). When he smiles his face's fatness hardens into little orbs and bulges of veined flesh, and his small, even teeth glint in warning. He is obsessed by the school's decline, because once – in the lifetime of the portraits hanging beside his – it had reputation. Their stares must be unbearable. The place has gone downhill in the insidious, half noticeable way that institutions do. A worse class of boy was attracting a worse type of teacher, he had told me when he hired me twenty years ago (Christ) and he meant to change all that.

But he never did. A fog of failure hangs over the staff – of failure not in their school duties, but in that they are here at all, in this cul-de-sac.

I, too. When I think that I came here to fill in time while deciding *what to do with my life*. In twenty years I've graduated to renting two rooms in the staff wing instead of one. I can play my Hi-Fi after ten o'clock without the assistant maths master banging on the wall with a shoe. Once McQuitty told me I was 'deputy-headmaster material'. I smiled back into those green eyes and felt my next twenty years, my whole life, being swallowed up. Then I went out and, literally, was sick down the lavatory.

Perhaps I'm a bit ill, have been ill ever since I was here. But what is my disease? I don't know. A girl-friend once called me an amoeba: I adapt myself so shamelessly to those around me that I come close to having no presence at all. Among the other masters I find myself agreeing with the most bigoted opinions, laughing at asinine jokes, yapping alongside all sorts of belligerence and stupidity. Don't ask me why. Yet I'm almost immorally sympathetic. I watch neurotically over the weaker and sadder schoolboys.

But the worst of it is that I'm starting to lose interest even in them. The time I feel most for them is at the start of a new term, when I notice the red-rimmed eyes of the seven- and eight-year olds – new initiates into this outdated hell, and victims (I suppose) of their parents' social ambition. The first few nights you can hear crying in the lower dormitories. Then come the whispers "Shut up, you squit!" from the tougher or senior ones, as if the whole caucus of boys were bunching itself together, disciplining itself for life, for hardness, for unfeeling.

But usually they seem more cohesive than we in the staff. They exist independent of us. Sometimes I envy them. Their lives aren't half over. I try to prepare them for things better than I've achieved. But all the time there's this gnashing inside me.

Why do I never try to get out? Years ago I used to scan the employment ads of *The Times Educational Supplement*. Sometimes I even wrote in, went for interviews. But I detest interviews. I used to feel myself freezing inside, physically freezing. I even tried imagining that my interviewer was not a person at all, but an automaton, powerless. I'd talk back as if to a machine. I'd feign indifference.

Yet my appearance is initially in my favour. I have the looks that many women are supposed to like. At least I did have ten years ago – dark hair and eyebrows and the big, saturnine eyes of my Jewish grandmother. I'm quite well-built. I give a plausible imitation of masculinity. But in the end this attractiveness only makes things worse. It's like a confidence trick. And besides, my interviewers were not women, but middle-aged men. They never gave me any time. Just as I was beginning to talk about something that interested me – the teaching of language, poetry – my interviewer would say "Well, thank you for coming, Mr Pashley. We'll be in touch. . . ."

I'm still here. The trouble is this place doesn't fit you for anything but itself. It's mercilessly complete. The walls circling the grounds are high (it used to be a convent) and everything inside them is embalmed. Past, present, future, they're all here. The future flows through our hands without leaving itself behind. Boys growing fast, as if by magic, on the substandard food. While the past fills the passages in photographs of school cricket teams decades old, sepia faces so callow that you wonder what can have become of them, so dazed by their future (killed in the war?) Only we teachers remain static. This is our world, where we're small kings. But you learn to loathe it. Sometimes I think we're afraid to look each other in the face. You want to break away, burst through, out. But it seems to be inside you now, and you can't. The boys all call you 'sir'. We are, they think, what they will become. But of course that's nonsense, because we're an aberration, only leftover schoolboys. And when they return as Old Boys, they stare into my face and say "Good heavens, it's old Pashers isn't it? You're still here!" Their voices rummage around the word 'sir'. But suddenly you look smaller, integrated into the real scale of things, and you imagine them going away, as big as you now, or bigger, and thinking: Christ, how odd. . . .

Sometimes I feel I'm going mad. It's as if the view from my room circumscribed the world – rotting goalposts, rhododendrons, glint of lake. Spring is the worst time, I don't know why. Christmas too – at Christmas I travel up to see my father and stepmother in Leeds. My father calls me Danny-boy, and says "How's the teaching going, old son, good, well, eh? Splendid!" all in one breath; but I sense a disappointment, unacknowledged even to himself, that his only son hasn't moved on. This is unbearable. "When's the headmastership falling vacant then? McQuitty must be getting on a bit. Fat as a pig, you say. Good subject for a heart attack, eh? Hah-hah! Didn't mean it. But when he retires. . . . Or perhaps you could try something different. . . ."

"Yes, I guess so, maybe." *Dad, I'm forty.*

What the hell happened to those years? Yet I'm still behaving as if they were a preparation, as if some different future lay beyond.

My stepmother married my father out of sheer, buxom tenderness. I think he is now what's meant by happy. He never talks of my mother.

"And are you getting married?" my stepmother demands. Marriage has been good to her.

"Haven't found the right girl. . . ."

Marriage. There aren't any girls at Sunningrove. It's as if they're excluded on purpose. Every one of the maids and cooks is elderly, and the young married masters live outside the grounds (so would I). I used to see a lot of a deputy matron called Beth. It caused a faint scandal, and she left years ago. I came to think I wasn't capable of love. My passions were diverted into teaching, books, music. I entertained fantasy women. That's what a place like this can do to you. Masturbation. Sports days to me were a panorama of parents' younger sisters. They would stand amused or bewildered beside the ribboned tracks and pennants, and talk with me because I was a master (and superficially good-looking) who might affect their nephew's future. I ached to fall in love. Love, after all, would be reality, the wrench out of isolation (and perhaps out of this detestable hole). If only I could have loved. I had fleeting affairs with two of those clear-faced younger sisters. I longed to lose myself. But each time, suddenly there came this panic: it was even physical, a contraction and coldness in my chest, as if some force had edged up out of my stomach. I've never reacted like other people. Beneath this pleasing (at least to women) exterior, something is blurring and disintegrating. Nobody can understand this who doesn't feel it. This fear seems not to be quite you. You can't control it. You've become unknown to yourself (of course you always were, but hadn't noticed). And even now I'm not explaining it. Even less, now.

I have no idea what I was protecting myself from, but for sex I started to choose (I realise this now) only women I didn't care for, or women who seemed subtly disqualified from my commitment – married women, older women. By the time I was thirty-one I had convinced myself that I was immune. An emotional eunuch.

That was why it came as such a shock.

Ten years ago, at the end of the Lent term, I was playing rugger with the senior fifteens, teaching them formation. I'm naturally athletic (another mask) and have the sinewy lightness of a long-distance runner. I remember I was running in mid-field, isolated. The boys were coming at me from both sides: a pair of thickset thirteen-year-olds to my left, a scrum of others to my right. Then an odd thing happened. Soft and hesitant at first, like the treble yap of puppies, then suddenly loud and united as if the whole pack had found its voice, there rose a long, harrowing shout: "Get 'im! Get 'im! Get 'im!" It was inexplicable, until I glanced to the touchline. And there was McQuitty, huge and red-faced, thumping his fist into the palm of his giant hand and bellowing: "Get 'im! Get 'im!" His mouth looked hot and swollen. My legs gave up. They simply turned to slow motion beneath me, as if I were driving a car which had run out of petrol. Somebody crashed against my thighs, another round my ankles. I fell, wincing and furious.

When I got up I found my left knee sprained. McQuitty's face had retreated to watchfulness, and his hands gone still. He shouted: "You've got 'em tackling good!"

I stumped up to him. Already I could feel my knee puffing up. "I've twisted something, Mr McQuitty. You'd better take over. I'm going to the clinic in Cruwenath."

I hate him. The whole school reeks of him.

But with each yard as I drove away down the yellow gravel track, reaching the lodge, the gates, the main road, the suffocating comfort of this place dropped behind. This always happens – a moment's release. Then the Outside hits you in a cold blast. It's a transition as precise as that – into a world where people inhabit adult horizons, make business decisions, talk in grown dialogue.

The waiting-room for afternoon surgery emptied while I glanced through magazines and read leaflets about baby care and V.D. Doctor Hughes-Davis, I remembered, was a caustic, middle-aged practitioner who usually dismissed or belittled his patients' pain. I imagine he'd been too long in his profession. Like me.

But when I entered the surgery he wasn't there. Behind his desk sat a woman doctor. Young. She looked up.

I don't really know how to go on writing this. The language is so soiled.

She was beautiful.

Yet I don't think it happened in me at once. Two minutes, perhaps, went by: two minutes in which I was slightly numbed, not feeling or thinking anything, just looking at her. Perhaps it was some bewitched kind of recognition. She asked my name, while her fingers flickered through a card-index. I wasn't there. So she stood and momentarily turned her back, reaching up for a file. If she hadn't done that, I might have survived.

But instead she left me with a picture of such sensuous shock that I was still staring when she turned round: simply her pale brown legs, cream-smooth, aglow with changing tendons. The tension of her tiptoe stance had lifted her calves into high, polished ovals and pulled her white skirt to close beneath the knee. Just where you would have expected a faint, shaved roughness, her skin flowed unbroken from leg into ankle, and in their flat shoes the blue-veined feet looked impossibly sensitised, their bones taut and fine like violin-strings. Yet these legs were nobody's cliché of perfection, not a model's legs, but absolutely individual – at once athletic, highstrung and tender – the kind of calves you long to smooth and knead in your fingers, cover with kisses.

"Mr Pashley? Ah, here's your card." She picked it from the file between slender fingers, the echo of those astonishing (and now invisible) legs. "Dr Hughes-Davis is away sick at the moment. What can I do for you?"

15

"I've gone and twisted my knee. Playing rugger. It's probably nothing much." My voice did not seem to have caught up with my feelings. It sounded extraordinarily matter-of-fact.

"May I look at it, please?"

I tried to pull up the leg of my jeans, but they were too narrow. I had to slide them off, and stood in my socks and shirt-tails. I felt gangling and foolish. My own legs looked spidery, flecked in their dark hairs, and seemed to taper feebly at the ankles. Even the knee was not heroically disfigured, only a little puffed and discoloured, slightly pathetic.

"How much weight can you put on it?" The next moment she was crouched in front of me, and I was looking down to where her chestnut hair grew shining and straight at the roots, before it tumbled into curls which she'd gathered in severely with a ribbon behind. And as her fingers probed the knee – "Does that hurt? No? Does this?" – I was unable to tell her if anything hurt, anything but some breathless core in me, and couldn't take my eyes from her fingers. Their flesh was spare and tight, the whole hand endlessly attenuated and graceful, even its nails pearly-thin, so that the touch and slide of each finger over the coarseness of my knee was separate and delicate, like a host of brown moths.

The voice below said: "You've torn a medial ligament." She stood up. "It's not serious. You'll need an elastic bandage and some ointment. Otherwise, just rest. If it hasn't gone down in a week, come back and we'll consider physiotherapy.."

The next moment one of those hands was holding out a prescription order, while the other rang a bell for the following patient. She gave me a smile of dismissal. But it was only like a seal on everything that had happened before. It irradiated what was already torturingly beautiful, as if she'd turned up the voltage on some inner dynamo of catastrophic power.

Out in Cruwenath high street, in the weak March sun, I stared through shop windows without understanding anything that was there. Even when objects were labelled 'Best cooking beef' or 'Fresh coffee bags' they remained ungraspable. The record and book shops confronted me simply with the idea that listening and reading were no longer relevant, but had been preparations for something else.

Every morning for a week afterwards, on the instant of waking, I would know that something was different, before its memory flooded in. This moment always amazed me. It was like waking with a strange face on the neighbouring pillow. I half expected it not to be there. Yes, in some part of me I was expecting the feeling to vanish as randomly and suddenly as it had arrived. For these few days the thing resembled a luxurious game. I didn't even know her name. I invented hundreds for her, but none seemed right. People coalesce around their names, but she – nameless – only grew more mysterious.

There is a primitive belief that without a name you don't exist.

By the end of the week the game had become frightening. She had rooted herself in my mind, flowered in its dark like a narcotic mushroom. There was nothing there but her, nameless her. I built her with the knowledge of imagination. She was unmarried and solitary. She took her holidays on the Continent, alone, she. . . . What was happening to me?

I pondered excuses for going back to the clinic. I watched in irritation as my swollen knee subsided. I had hopes of an inflamed ankle ligament, but it came to nothing. I thought of claiming a cartilaginous sprain, but I had rubbed in her prescribed ointment with religious tenderness, and the joint looked perfectly normal. It was not until I was inside the surgery that I almost panicked. When I picked up a magazine, it trembled. My face had gone bloodless and I had a sensation of ants trickling over my scalp. I was dressed with planned casualness, and where my hair was receding I had combed it forward in two easy-looking strands. Yet when my turn came my legs felt stiff and light. They might have been made for somebody else. I had prepared a lie about knee cartilages; it evaporated as I fumbled through the doorway.

But when I came in, the room seemed cold. It was filled only

17

with a pallid light from nowhere in particular, and by Dr Hughes-Davis at the desk. After his illness he looked still more desiccated and impatient than I remembered, and I had the illusion that he was translucent, like the light in the room. He dismissed my knee with contempt. As for the 'lady doctor', as he called her, she came from the Moore Street clinic at the other end of town. Women swamped the profession now, he added, and would I ask the next patient to come in?

For over an hour I waited in my car in Moore Street, planning what to do, calculating when she would go on her rounds. I framed her clinic's door in my side-mirror, and watched. I felt no trace of shame. Only fear and strangeness. I kept breaking into sweat. I even wondered if I would recognise her. For a whole week I had done little but daydream and remember, so that in my mind her portrait was painted over and retouched a hundred times. The door became the empty frame for someone unimaginable. By ten-thirty the trickle of departing patients had run dry. She must be filling in prescription forms. Even my hands were clammy. I had no idea what to do.

By eleven o'clock I grew restless. A little frightened of myself, I walked to the street corner and ambled down the pavement past the clinic. I could hear nothing inside. But on a plaque against the door I read her name.

I stopped, gazed. *Sophia*. It was soft, dignified. I wondered why I had not guessed it. But the noble Christian name was attended by a Sancho Panza of a surname: Brown. Dr Sophia Brown. I read it over soundlessly. Already I felt *Sophia* taking on the cadence of my passion, separating itself off from other names. Even in *Brown* I started to discern a maternal importance.

Then the door opened and she was standing less than three feet from me. All the fragments of memory flew together in her face.

"Doctor . . . Brown, isn't it?"

"I'm sorry, I've forgotten . . ."

"Daniel Pashley." I was stuttering. "Last week. The other clinic."

"Yes, I remember." Her smile was perfunctory, meaningless, radiant. "You tore your knee ligament. Is it better?"

Then we were walking side by side down the street, which was perfectly natural yet also extraordinary, and I was noticing how she moved – with springy steps – and I was joining this walk, this person and this name together. Yet I knew that she must be making for one of the cars parked along the street, and that I had no time at all. My voice sounded miles away. "Would you like some coffee?"

"I'm afraid I can't. I've got patients to see all morning."

"Would you have lunch then? Even you must eat."

She hesitated. Her astonishing blue gaze flickered over me, wondering.

The voice that used to be mine added: "Say yes."

"I'd only have an hour."

"An hour then." *An hour.* My autonomous voice continued: "The Alpina. One o'clock."

She had reached her car. "All right." She opened the door, then as if regretting some gracelessness, said: "Fine. Thank you."

A moment later I was standing on the pavement alone, delirious, hardly believing the thing's simplicity.

I don't understand Time. There have been years at Sunningrove of which I recall nothing. But from that one hour with Sophia the memories swim up now with a pristine, terrible brightness, so that I can feel the airiness in my chest and stomach, the torment of the shortening minutes, the insane glory of that face, the irrelevance of everything else. It was not exactly happy. Happiness suggests too much of the carefree. Rather, it contained a frightening, exquisite intensity.

The little restaurant must have been noisy, and our table was crowded by others. But for me her presence threw transparent walls round us, muffling everything outside. All the time I was with her I felt slightly sick, slightly faint, yet so impressible that I could have heard an ant breathe.

She had a quality of haunting directness. All the time she spoke her eyes were fixed on mine with absolute attention.

They were the most extraordinary, vivid blue, wide-spaced under wide brows, and they radiated a candid brilliance. I was suffused and drowned in them. In fact when I held their gaze for long I felt I was committing a kind of suicide. I became helpless. She seemed to be reeling me in along her eye-beams like a fish. Perhaps it was the contrasting brownness of her skin which lent them this odd, pale incandescence, or the exotic darkness of her eyebrows above. I don't know. Her whole person was quicksilver. She had released her hair into jostling curls around her shoulders. Whenever she laughed or moved, these curls shifted and glistened about her neck. Her smile had the same effect: like an intensification of light. In repose, her lips were full and firm, and her expression was turned faintly austere by the sculptural tautness of her cheeks under their high bones. But the next moment the breaking of her smile would redistribute her beauty's emphasis, as if by the shake of some internal kaleidoscope, so that I would be caught staring and dazed by her.

For the first twenty minutes I was too drugged by her to do more than banter, apologise for my boldness, order the wrong wine and ask questions about her medical practice. But little by little I pieced this precious life together. She came from the West Country, where her mother still lived, and she must, I calculated, be twenty-nine. She'd never been married. She'd passed out high from medical school, but had chosen not to specialise. If the top graduates always specialised, she said, general practice became impoverished. I already sensed a reticent social conscience, and I admired it as I might admire a star, without being able to share in it at all. She even asked me about this in her frank, sudden way, and I could only say: "I couldn't be a doctor. I'm no good at loving people *en masse*."

"Who said anything about *love*? No, no." She laughed. "You soon lose all that."

Then she was asking me about my job. I felt frantic with shame. I said that it was temporary, that I planned to leave, that I would teach in public schools, serve on local educational committees. I lied shamelessly. I was writing a book, I said, I had a publisher interested. Then something broke in me.

"I can't tell you what a hell Sunningrove is. The junior kids especially – that's psychological massacre. They come in quite gentle, and then the place gets them. Sometimes I just cut off. At the start of last term I was on Newport station when one of the eight-year-olds was being sent off. He had to be tricked from his mother's arms. It was like an execution. That night they were whimpering like puppies in the dormitories." My talking sounded fast and breathless. "But what's the point of it? What's it for?"

"Did you suffer like that yourself?"

"Are you doing a psychiatric job on me?"

She laughed. I desperately wanted to touch her. Her hands were resting by her plate, the hands which had healed my knee: fine-spun fingers, I daren't take them.

"Why do you stay at this school, then? Why don't you leave?"

Why don't I? She made it sound simple – and yes, *she* would have achieved it long ago. "Well, I suppose you get attached in the end. Some of the boys. A few of the masters . . ." *Liar* "But I'm not staying much longer. I've come to the end, really I have." I believed this at the time. I was talking to myself as well as her. It was a relief to be honest. But I perpetually wondered how I seemed in her eyes. Towards the end of our hour I heard myself talking about Berlioz and Mahler in a rush of enthusiastic inaccuracy. I suppose I wanted her to think me learned. She answered through her strange gift of concentrated attention, and I sat in the blue tide of her gaze and talked on and on about symphonies and operas I loved but of which she (I later realised) had never heard. Yet something about her stillness made me go on. I was talking in a way I hadn't anticipated, and it was luxurious to pour these disordered loves into her lap – Berlioz, Dostoevsky, picnics in the Lucanian hills, Sicilian orchards – and to find her face not mocking at all, but seeming to extend to me a kind of austere tenderness (I can't really explain it) peculiar to herself.

I still wonder what she saw.

As the time moved to its hour, she glanced at her watch but didn't immediately go. She said: "You haven't eaten a *thing*.

Don't you usually?" It was true, I'd merely rearranged my cannelloni and pulverised a lemon sorbet. My stomach was contracted to nothing. "Doesn't your girlfriend feed you?"

I winced in the laser-beam stare. I thought: if I say I'm alone, I'll seem unwanted. But I could no longer lie to her. I felt an appalled instinct for confession. "I don't have one." I started to blush like a teenager, tried to joke. "I'm not much good in that direction." *Sounds as if I'm impotent.* "I mean I don't seem to have been, it always falls to bits. . . . I don't know." I couldn't look at her. "I'm not explaining properly. What about your boyfriend?"

Tell me he doesn't exist.

"Oh I don't cook for *him*. He's very capable."

Something bright and hallucinatory shattered and re-assembled in me, composing itself greyer and sadder but more solid than before. Then she added: "He lives on his own."

Weakly, filling in silence, I said: "What does he do?"

"He's a house agent."

"Oh."

Her voice surrounded him with no special tone. I tried to picture him, but couldn't. The man who slept with that body. I tried to force the fact on myself. I stared at her. Under her blue pullover her breasts were high and small. I couldn't imagine him with them. Perhaps, unconsciously, I was claiming them for myself. I imagined their naked shape. I had always been attracted by heavy breasts, but now these soft buds became perfect, simply because they were hers. It was as if this dazed adoration, and this utter inability to imagine the house agent, had subsumed sexual jealousy altogether. Perhaps that was why, as we emerged onto the street outside, I could ask her to come out to dinner one evening and she could accept. She wrote down the date in a pocket diary full of other engagements, but its presence there at all – 'Daniel 7.30' – struck me as a miracle.

As I turned in through the dilapidated gates of Sunningrove, I waited for the familiar depression to descend. The long gravel snake of the drive hissed its warning under my tyres, and

22

the rhododendrons banked alongside in a dead audience. But Sophia had even written her address and telephone number on a scrap of paper now folded in my jacket pocket. I touched it like an amulet: it turned everything else to dust or sunlight. I was singing aloud, laughing. As the brick palisade of class-rooms and dormitories loomed into sight I whooped derisively and stuck out my tongue.

It was rest-hour and the corridors were empty. I noticed with surprise how the sun poured against the scarred panelling of the passageways, mellowing them into long, tiger-striped vistas. It must always have done that, I thought, and I'd never noticed. In my classroom somebody had chalked on the blackboard in official-looking capitals: "Please do not feed the form master". I laughed and left it there. Outside the window, beyond the playing-fields, the lake shone glassy-bright. This view had depressed me for years, but now seemed curiously diffused and thinned. It was as if something, or somebody, had abandoned it. I wondered why it had once seemed to circle me, and to rise so close, so dense, and why I had imagined you could see the high surrounding walls from here. It seemed neuter now. Nothing.

That evening I poured down in writing everything Sophia and I had said to one another. I think I remembered every sentence, however fleeting. I described her appearance, even her tiny blemishes – the faint, opaque crescents under her eyes, the feathery mirage of hair above her lip, the start of lines across her forehead. I tabulated her different kinds of laughter, the peculiar inflections she had given to some remarks, what she might have been thinking. I hunted ravenously for any sign that she liked me, and found a few cherished phrases and accents (which I underscored in red.) I scribbled these heaps of notes in a rushed passion, and finished them late at night, exhausted and suddenly relieved as if I only now possessed that unaccountable hour.

But I wondered what on earth she had seen. I stared in the mirror and encountered this astonishing deception – a thirty-one-year-old man, with dark good looks and emotional eyes. Sometimes only my eyes strike me as mine.

I lay awake a long time, planning how to emancipate myself, find a more prestigious job, buy my own place. It was almost dawn before I fell asleep, swearing to myself: *I'll get out of here*.

I dreamed of her, sexlessly, a very simple dream – nothing really. We were walking together down a dark passageway at whose end a frosted glass door emitted faint light. I said "It's quite a long way." But she leaned her head against my shoulder with an odd gentleness and answered "That's all right." This sounds trivial, I know. It was the power of feeling that made it so strange: I woke up weeping. Sometimes I don't understand myself at all. Or anything.

A few days later the school broke up for the short spring holiday. Most of the masters who lived on the premises remained, loitering in the library and food halls, feeling excluded from some life imagined elsewhere. In these days we all seemed visibly to shrivel, as if the boys had stolen our sense of self. The silence became an accuser. Our occasional laughter crashed like dropped plates. Even the old history master Nisbet, my favourite, would say querulously: "It's hard to feel whole without them, isn't it? But that's right, you know. Teaching is a calling. All the same, one does feel rather – how can I put it? – ghostly here. . . ."

I spent my time scouring the 'situations vacant' columns. But my typed *curriculum vitae* looked so wretched that I tore it up and tried to compose letters. The posting of these was agony. The idea of interviews started me shaking. Literally. It was like being naked in a hailstorm, and from that time to this I've never exposed myself again. I simply can't take them, and there's an end of it. I can't. Anyway, I don't think I'm fitted for change. And there's no need now.

For a while, in any case, Sunningrove didn't seem so bad any more. It no longer imprisoned; it merely spread around with an exorcised drabness. The prospect of dinner with Sophia would have immunised me against Hell. I prepared for it days beforehand. I booked the most intimate table in an expensive restaurant in Monmouth – a romantic drive twenty minutes away over the hills. I overhauled my car and even decided on my clothes. Once I made a covert trip to her home, a russet-stoned cottage on the edge of Cruwenath, and gazed over its fence at a garden of newly-planted shrubs.

Later came a mingled fear and exhilaration. Something must surely go wrong? I purposely imagined disasters in order to forestall them, since things envisaged never seem to happen – she'd be ill and unable to come; she'd have forgotten altogether and gone out; a patient would be dying and need her; her boyfriend. . . .

But when the time came, the cottage door opened on a woman of whom my remembered image had only been a wraith. This gulf between the imagined and the real never stopped amazing me with her. It happened again and again. And the astonishing thing was that my image was always less poignant, less intense, than her reality, as if in the intervals between our meeting my mind had refused quite to believe in her, and had tried to shade her back a little into ordinariness. As for the genuine, tiny changes in her, they always seemed dazzlingly emphatic. Even as I stood on the doorstep, there began a hectic quest to absorb all the little differences – a flush of rouge along her cheekbones, a suspicion of scent, her white silk blouse which framed a new part of her body (the softness of the neck where it met her shoulders) – and a subtly different mood, she more relaxed, more pleased.

We drove to Monmouth in my clapped-out Morris while the Black Mountains rose about us bare as bones and blacker even than the sky. I listened to her talking in that orchestra of a voice, commenting blithely on the night landscape.

As we parked outside the restaurant she said: "That looks rather expensive. Why don't we got to a bistro?"

I realised that she disapproved, but heard myself say bleakly: "I've booked."

She must have seen my face. She was impulsively apologetic: "Oh what the hell? I didn't mean to sound like that." She peeled off her coat in the lobby. Beyond its glass doors radiated soft lights and subdued, expensive chatter. For a minute we paused in front of them to stare up at a framed menu. And then there occurred one of those moments – unnoticeable to an outsider – which seem only the more private and intimate for happening in public. I was standing behind her, no longer in that searing gaze – and I think it was because of this that I dared to rest my fingertips gently on her shoulders. Then gently, helplessly, I began to probe their tight, luxurious flesh, making love to the warm skin through the thin silk, feeling down to arms soft and lithe with female muscle, and down again to clasp her cool hands. It was the first time I'd ever touched her. For half a minute, perhaps, she remained tense and separate in my arms, her back turned, then softly, deliberately, she arched herself against me in an act of unmistakable acceptance, until the calves of her legs were pressing against mine, her hair brushed my neck and her small buttocks nested to my thighs. Yet so slight and natural was this movement that our faces were still turned sightlessly to the menu, and two or three clients passed by without a glance.

The moment released us. Our supper became a gale of exchanges and enthusiasms. She began a humorous description of medical school, grew pessimistic and passionate about her profession, became momentarily angry at the menu prices ("*Look* at that, no I *won't* have scallops") and gave an exuberant catalogue of the spring-flowering shrubs in her garden. Gardens took us to the Continent and to my holidays back-packing along the Moselle, up the Rhine, through the Black Forest. And all the time, pinioned by those blue eyes, I was sure that the love was pouring like sweat from my face. Hadn't she noticed?

But I was permeated by fear too. Fear and love seemed inseparable. Her power over me was horrifying. With other women I'd felt guilty for not feeling enough; but with her I was terrified at feeling so much. Terrified and exalted. Twice I was so distracted by her that I blurted out questions while she was talking about something quite different. Once I even asked: "Why haven't you married?" (she pretended that nobody had asked her) and once, dazed by her skin's darkness in the muted light: "Have you been away?"

She frowned. "What on *earth's* that got to do with it? No I haven't. Why?"

26

"I thought you'd been on holiday, sunbathing."

"No, my skin's always this dirty beige." She glanced at her hands with strange distaste. "I don't like lying on beaches – after a while I start to twitch. I ought to take your sort of trips and 'do the South German baroque' or 'cover the Italian Romanesque'. I really ought." She seemed to mean it. "Instead I end up in Cornwall or the Algarve."

"Why?" Indescribable holidays with her were unwinding behind my eyes.

"I don't know. I suppose it's the people I've been with. They haven't been interested."

"Who are these people?" I tried to sound casual.

"Oh, men."

I listened for feeling in the words, and thought I heard a faint regret. I couldn't imagine these holidays, these men. But I could imagine her nakedness now. She seemed suddenly accessible. My longing for the white silk breasts had been hot and present all the time. I said: "If I were on holiday with you" – and the banal words seemed to create the possibility – "I'd forget the German baroque."

I scoured her face. It had turned pensive. For a second we stared across the table at one another in silence. I had asked, in all but the words, to go away with her, and for this fatal, fleeting instant, I am sure, she was genuinely considering what I'd said. Then I heard my voice, tiny, involuntary, add: "*Please.*"

For ten yers now I've regretted that whispered monosyllable. It was so importunate, too pleading. Her mouth smiled; but two tiny, vertical lines jerked into prominence between her eyes. Her voice came self-consciously airy: "Have you never gone away with anyone?"

"Oh, years ago once." *Beth: willing myself to fall in love.* "And last year with Nisbet, our history master. He's elderly and a bit frail, but we're interested in Gothic architecture." My voice rushed on, saddened. "Years ago I used to go away with my father. We both enjoy wild scenery. We even came to Wales."

"That's why I chose a practice here," she said. "The wildness." As if to compensate for something, she leaned forward and touched my hand. "Do you want to come for a walk on

27

Saturday? There's a tributary of the Usk runs almost through my garden. Are you free?"

The sudden tenderness of this hand, laid like an exquisite apology over mine, would have reconciled me to death. "Yes, I'm free."

The hand withdrew. She said: "Are your parents country people too?"

"My father, yes."

"Your mother?"

"She was a garden-lover."

Softly: "Is she dead?"

Is she? In a way. Yes, she is.

"Yes, she is."

"A long time ago?"

Yes, long ago.

"Yes."

A garden lover. Gazing at a snake in the flower-bed, slithered there to swallow frogs. Her eyes look strange. I run against her lap, frightened. "Little idiot, it's not an adder. It's just a slow-worm, a legless lizard." Smiling for once: the piercing eyes that went cold. "You like lizards."

She stood up to leave. I was momentarily astonished that everybody's head didn't turn to fall in love with her. But nobody seemed to look at her particularly. Except me.

The next few days were ludicrously happy. The summer term began. The younger masters joked that 'the monk', as they called me, was going about so elated that he must have been breaking his vows. I taught my classes with a new zest. By the time Saturday arrived the morning grammar lesson had flowered into a theatre of nine-year-olds impersonating relative and conditional clauses. ("Pashley's going bonkers," I overheard. "*Going?*")

The one person with whom I could share my feelings was Nisbet. I found him alone early that afternoon, dozing in the masters' common room. He'd had cancer the year before, and looked far older than his fifty-nine years. His body was thin as paper, and his skin glassy white. No collar was close-fitting enough to hug the skeletal neck. It seemed to uphold his head only by a trick of balance, and the workings of his Adam's Apple made the boys squeal. Behind their thick-lensed spectacles, which lent him a subaqueous vacancy, the brown eyes were intelligent and a little melancholy, but now, in sleep, closed by empurpled lids, their absence left his face quite expressionless. I padded over to the record-player. He and I shared a passion for Bach and Haydn, but he hated anything twentieth century. I put on *The Song of the Earth* to provoke him.

"How *can* you?" He shook his head awake. "Mahler! Oh, ugh." The pedantic voice seemed to have risen an octave in the abruptness of his waking up. He straightened his waistcoat. "You've had a devil in you recently. For months you spend all your spare time in your room, and then suddenly you're everywhere – singing, buffooning, making everybody feel – how can I put it? – somewhat uncomfortable." But he was smiling. "Mahler. Aagh. What is it then, what's got into you? Something has."

I sat beside him. "Is it that obvious?"

"Yes. Yes, I would say so. At least to me." He patted my chair-arm in lieu of my hand. He looked pleased, yet regretful. "Tell me then: which school are we losing you to?"

"*School*?"

"Yes, dear boy. Isn't it that? You've been offered another post?"

I burst into laughter. "Oh no, no, nothing of the sort. It's a *woman*."

I waited for his surprise and pleasure, but instead his thin knees closed together and his face clouded into bafflement. "I confess I had no idea of that. None at all." His gaze on me was suddenly vague, as if I were much farther away. "I hope she's what's called suitable."

"She's a doctor in Cruwenath."

He frowned faintly. "Not a Doctor Brown?"

"Yes! Do you know her?" He seemed instantly different, transfigured with a new stature and interest.

29

"No alas, I only encountered her professionally, as it were. Last year I found I had an allergy to aspirin, developed lumps along the spine and so forth. It was certainly Doctor Brown who treated me. I remember the name."

I was experiencing the titillation of discussing the loved one, hearing her name, seeing her through another's eyes. Not that anything anybody said could change a shred of what I felt. It was simply a voluptuous game, a by-product of passion. "So what did you think of her?"

"Oh, she seemed most efficient. She prescribed Piriton, I think . . ."

"But *her*. What of *her*?"

"I really can't remember very much." He frowned. "I dare say she was quite pretty."

I writhed. 'Pretty' described ornaments, not people. "You *must* remember."

"I'm sorry." He shook his head. "I can't have noticed."

"Oh God, don't you *like* women?"

But I instantly regretted this. His head wavered on its neck like a topheavy flower, and a constricted coughing started from his throat. "It's not precisely a matter of liking or disliking. . . ." His voice rose quavering, estranged, then a new spasm of coughing hit him, and he stopped.

Something I'd already half known came suddenly into focus. Nisbet, fastidious, self-disciplined, normally so rational, would occasionally call a boy 'beautiful'. Yet even now, with the flush from his cheeks, he was oddly dignified. How was I to know what his self-respect had cost him?

I didn't know what to say. "I'm a bit carried away by her. I'm so sorry." But through the windows the sun shone warm in a clear sky, and it was the afternoon of our walk. I got up to go.

Nisbet looked up at me. "I hope it goes well for you, Daniel." His hand delayed me. His tongue was flickering round his lips, preparing them for difficult words. My blundering had enabled him to risk a blunder too. "Please forgive me for saying this, but sometimes, I must confess, you worry me. I feel you are a little – how can I put it? – emotionally

30

unstable. Romantic, you know. Do forgive me. There are such strong forces in us all, too strong. I'm afraid I'm not explaining myself at all."

But I'd forgotten him by the time I'd reached Cruwenath. The hills round here are lonely, with a few white farmhouses scattered along their slopes. A tributary of the Usk clatters down through a tree-crowded valley which rises to uplands of sheep pasture and the bald heads of the beacons. But I shall never love this country.

I was apprehensive the moment I saw another car outside her gate. As I arrived she emerged from the door with a man and a girl, and my heart sank. They were dressed for walking. We all shook hands. "This is Daniel . . . Daniel, this is Angela Stainton . . . this is Charles. . . ." The next moment we were making for the river, chatting, trying to decide on each other. In Sophia's manner was no hint that she'd ever meant to walk alone with me. It had simply been my fantasy. The expression on her face was blithe, calm. Her blue anorak echoed her eyes. Whereas I felt such a sudden, overwhelming tiredness that I wondered if I'd be able to walk far at all.

The river enclosed us in trees. It came down from a red upland earth and dropped through the wildness in auburn-tinted pools. The whole valley was a staircase of shallow cascades. Great oaks and beeches writhed even from the water, or bound the soil into miniature, stranded headlands, where they lurched and tilted together or had fallen across the water to form bridges for hikers and sheep.

"Pretty, isn't it?" said Charles.

He and Angela were brother and sister. They shared the same look of bland pleasantness. They were blond and pale-eyed and somehow out-of-focus. I wondered who was meant for who. Was I supposed to pair off with Angela? She strode beside me, big-boned; Charles and Sophia a few paces behind. Perhaps it was Angela's Guernsey sweater or Charles's heavy, leather-elbowed sports jacket which suggested class; or perhaps the woodland silence which exaggerated the remnant of

31

my Northern accent. In any case, they weren't typical of Cruwenath. Had they come from the south-east, I asked Angela?

No, said Charles from behind. His voice held an odd, rasping tone. Their family owned a house agency in Monmouth, he said. He was a house agent.

I suddenly didn't want to look behind me. I don't know how I knew, but his arm was round her shoulders. I shut my eyes and was engulfed by sickness. Trapped somewhere in my chest, high under my throat, an animal's cry was contained and suffocated.

Dimly I was aware of Charles's voice. "The property market's got a busy spell on at the moment. . . . Plenty of the right stuff coming in. . . ." He came alongside me, his hands in his pockets now. "The drop in mortgage interest rates hasn't done us any harm either. Turnover's double what it was last year. . . ."

He talked on and on while I listened. My misery was suppressed in the fever of assessing him, and all the time I heard the rustle of Sophia's boots over last year's leaves a yard behind us. But he talked only in clichés. I couldn't discover him. And it was the same when I looked at him. He was conventionally handsome, I could see: yet suppressed, unlit. Only the odd, rasping voice didn't fit the stereotype which he inhabited. His heavy-lidded eyes gave him a look of sleepy superiority. He might have been blurred in mist. Utter bewilderment crept over me – mingled relief and unease. The grotesque discrepancy between him and Sophia plunged me into wonderment as to what she saw, needed. Was he just good in bed? I was furiously jealous – but of a ghost. His arm had circled her casually, as of right – and he could afford his detachment if she loved him, he was in the complacency of paradise. He might be less than her, but he was more than me. Cruelly, definitively, more. I observed his long stride, his height. He projected a certain mute strength. His features were straight, very regular. Whereas I – my gait was impetuous and unco-ordinated. I've never had any poise.

His conversation was filled with business jargon and

metaphors, which I started to loathe. I wondered how Sophia bore it. If she were to accept his marriage proposal, I could imagine him calling it a 'turn-up for the book'. If she refused, he'd 'seek alternative outlets'.

I debated how often they'd followed this stream together. He seemed to know the way. It was beautiful, and I hated it. I tried to detach it from him while he went on speaking. After all, it was really hers. She was walking behind with Angela. I could feel her eyes on us. I couldn't keep in step with him along the path. Now he was talking about the effect on housing of a population shift from the Midlands. His words had a colourless authority. I kept foolishly agreeing with them. My voice sounded breathless and high. Conversation between Sophia and Angela petered out.

We came into a glen where the stream slipped between high rocks glazed in moss and dripping ferns. An old carter's bridge, where a track once crossed, had left behind a crumbling arch whose base had been gouged by the current into liquid black caves. And perched in a neighbouring beech, as if to complete the drama of the place, a dark, dwarf bird with a rounded head was silhouetted.

"Newly-marrieds snap up anything around the £20,000 mark," Charles was saying, "but if you want a four-bedroom unit . . ."

"Look!" I said. "A tawny owl."

We all stopped. Sophia was standing between us now. "Where?" She followed my gaze: a tiny, foolish victory. The owl remained motionless, perched closed to the trunk. But I could see that its black eyes were wide open in their feathered discs. It was watching us.

"That's not a tawny," Charles said, "that's a wood owl."

I snapped: "They're the same thing." He didn't know about owls. Owls weren't on the market.

"Oh, right," he said pleasantly. "Over to you."

I took him at his word. I started talking about everything around us which his own monologue had contaminated – owls, trees, ferns, lichens (I misnamed them), the fantastical tree-roots, the rock strata, the changing colour of the river, the beauty of its stones. My voice made a thin prattle in the silence. It grew foolishly impassioned about kingfishers. It sounded at once pedantic and puerile – the product of my bloody job, I thought helplessly. Nobody answered. Charles and Angela struck out as if they were on military exercise, and although Sophia glanced at me from time to time, I never dared meet her gaze. I could imagine my gaucheness, my irrelevance, in her eyes. I knew my face must be dead white. It felt wooden, out-of-joint, like a slipping mask. I couldn't even walk straight. And all he had to do was to stride in front of me in that expensive sports-jacket and let me condemn myself. I bitterly despised and envied him. I was starting to sweat. (Yes, I know this was all adolescent, I know. But that's how passion was.)

It was Angela who noticed the sodden fur among the stream's stones. The rabbit lay where the rocks made a shallow causeway, its nose inches from the dry land, inexplicably drowned. The gentle current had twisted its neck downstream.

She pulled it ashore. Its eyes were blackly open. "I think it's still alive."

We stared down at it. One leg was broken, but the other three twitched. "How extraordinary." Charles knelt by it. "Poor little thing. They're really rather beautiful, aren't they?" But the words came inflated and unnatural from him. I had an idea that he was taking his tone from me, parodying me in front of Sophia.

I said brusquely: "Hind leg's broken. It hasn't a hope." I was relieved to find my voice lower, steadier. "You can't worry about it, when the farmers round here are trying to control vermin."

"All the same." He stroked its flank nauseously with the back of his hand. "When you see them like this, in pain . . ." He was pretending sensitivity. Sophia was leaning above it now, her hands on her knees, and I realised that his words were meant for her. The rabbit was nothing.

"We can't leave it here," she said. "Something will get it."

I looked around us for a place to lay the creature, and redeem my betrayal of it; but there was nowhere safe. The glen was close and sunless, filled with a greenish light. On a boulder by the stream's edge stood a black cigarette packet, empty, un-explained, as if somebody had sat there smoking while the rabbit drowned.

Sophia said: "It's kinder to kill it." One of her hands stretched out to confirm the broken leg, and I was surprised to see her eyes moist. Charles still knelt melodramatically beside her, while I stood above with my hands in my pockets in an attitude of indifference. I detested us both. Then we all moved away, leaving Charles to kill it.

Sophia had subtly detached herself. She walked with Angela a long way ahead. Charles and I drifted together and strolled in part-silence. Sometimes I had the impression that he wanted to ask me something, that he was even a little pathetic. But too much dishonesty had passed. At other times he appeared to be feeling sorry for me. There were things I longed to ask him (I even framed a facetious remark about wedding-bells) but the questions paralysed me almost as I conceived them.

By the time I left, Sophia and I had barely exchanged a word. I drove back to Sunningrove feeling exhausted. There was a note pinned to my door. It read: 'Come and see me at once. McQuitty.' This demand would normally have filled me with alarm, but for an hour I sat jaded in my room scribbling down impressions from that walk. Then I fingered through my diary of past meetings with Sophia – everything we'd said – but it only depressed me. It seemed curiously ordinary.

McQuitty's study was like an inquisition chamber. At the end of its narrow bareness stood an enormous desk whose lamp flooded his victim's face while shadowing his own. His tie was wrenched askew beneath an open-necked shirt, as if he were aping a journalist before deadline; and because his face was half in shadow the terrible, coarse impatience of the man seemed mounded in his bullish shoulders and flatulent neck. But it is none of these things that personify him for me. Instead it is an insistent aural memory: a dry, regular rapping which was the barometer of his temper. All McQuitty's intolerance seemed concentrated in this staccato report of his knuckles

on the desk-top, so that you waited for the rap-rap-rap of
his signet-ring finger like a tocsin. It was the very sound of
fear.

It began the moment I entered the study. I think this was
conscious sadism. But I waited for the familiar quaking in me,
and was distantly surprised that it didn't come. For the only
time in my life I looked at McQuitty with no feeling at all,
other than a certain curiosity about the pulse-beat of the
knuckles. The backlit head, I thought, was balder than I'd ever
noticed. Its rusty hair now circled a pate like the flat base of a
ham.

"So where do we think we've been this afternoon?" he
demanded. He used the 'we' to rob his victims of their presence:
but I felt absent in any case.

"In Cruwenath."

"In Cruwenath." He repeated "In Cruwenath", as if it were
Sodom. Already the intervals were shortening between the
raps of his knuckles. "And you didn't by any chance have any
feeling . . . any feeling that you'd *forgotten* anything?"

"No."

Rap-rap-rap. "You don't recall that you were meant to be
supervising the upper fourth's detention? No. Instead you left
them to create bedlam. Bedlam! I could hear the noise ten walls
away!"

I had completely forgotten. Sophia had obliterated it. "I do
apologise . . ."

"We do apologise, do we? And who d'we think had to cope
with the bedlam?"

Rap-rap-rap. Then he exploded. All the polished roundels of
his face – cheeks, chin, brows – suddenly crashed and bumped
together. "I had to *myself! Myself*, do you know? *Myself!*" The
pronoun seemed to hold special significance for him.

I was fascinated by my own coolness. I was watching him
with dissociated wonder, imagining him through the eyes of a
schoolboy, myself even, and remembering how the adult
body had seemed something I would never attain to: something
foreign, unbecomable. Now I stared at McQuitty's hands and
wondered how a boy could ever imagine owning them, with

their piggy, pale red hairs and their fingers bulging like strings of red sausages.

I said: "Mr McQuitty, I've been teaching here for over nine years [Hell!] and this is the first time I've . . ."

"It's not only today!" The rapping started up again, but he looked fleetingly surprised by my composure. "It's all this term. You've not been pulling your weight. Well, have you?"

"I've . . ."

"No! You suddenly proved yourself thoroughly unreliable! What's been wrong with you these last weeks?"

The next moment, to my astonishment, I'd said: "I've fallen in love."

It was an absurd thing to tell McQuitty: like telling a boa-constrictor your ribs were delicate. His mouth became a cynical slit. "Be your age!"

Even my anger was aloof, restrained, "Don't patronise me, Mr McQuitty. My feelings aren't for you to judge."

I had never heard anyone speak to him like that before. But I realised, as I watched the disconcert in that face, that there was nothing more he could do. His rages were no more than the self-induced explosions of a sergeant-major. He used them professionally, like weapons. But now, as if I had burst through some invisible barrier and was out into calm beyond, he could only show sarcasm and a face-saving bombast which ended: "You can go now. *Romeo*."

The happiest memories are the least bearable now. It was the kind of evening which you later imagine full of sunlight – the sort of golden wash obtained by underexposed film. Its spurious halo surrounds her.

She could wear the most unappealing clothes and transfigure them. She came to the door dressed in an orange apron and holding a potato-peeler. On her kitchen draining-board were little piles of sliced mushroom, tomato, liver, parsley, so carefully prepared that I asked her in foolish surprise: "Was that done for me?"

"Yes of course."

I could never absorb the rush of things with her, and now she threw off the apron from her summer dress – and the high profile of her breasts – and we wandered through the ordered informality of the sitting-room which I'd never seen (Indian wall-hangings, thumbed paperbacks, dried foliage) and out into her garden.

She said at once: "You didn't like Charles, did you?" It was more like a confidence than a question.

"I found him difficult. Stiff, that's all. He found me difficult too."

Silence. There was a sickening kind of waiting in the air. For all I knew she'd start the next sentence 'when he and I get married . . .' We walked to the garden's end, where a stagnant goldfish pond was filled with leaves. She said: "You and he are quite different."

"*Yes*."

"Why do you say it like that?"

"How did I say it?"

"As if you, he . . . oh hell . . . He worries you, doesn't he?"

Then a small, extraordinary thing happened. Her hands came up and cupped my cheeks as if she were about to kiss me. It sounds nothing, I know. But she had this unique gift for deepening (so it seemed) into a sudden tenderness. All at once she would intensify and soften. And the change was concentrated, I was sure, in those unearthly eyes, as if it were some expression in the irises or pupils themselves which altered.

I crouched down like a coward by the pool. "Yes, he does worry me." I pretended to be looking for tadpoles. A few lily pads stirred above the bed of drowned leaves. I felt slightly sick. The water shone with a glaze of insects. She remained standing above me. The brown calves of her legs were poised and nervous, their tendons shifting. I looked up and saw the blue-veined hand, absolutely still against the blue dress, its slim-nailed fingers tense. And on one finger was a ring.

On the marriage finger.

I stared. A small diamond on a silver band. It lent the hand

38

atrocious beauty. My fingers reached out to grasp hers, and I stood up, lifting it. "What's this?"

She looked at me then burst into laughter. "Oh Daniel!" She tugged the ring off. "I just wear this for my patients. Some of the men get ideas . . . I seem to attract the over-forties." Her laughter vanished into the long, apologetic smile of her eyes, her head thrown back a little against its cataract of hair. "You idiot." Her mouth became a see-saw of derision and sympathy.

I stared at her, dazed. Then a surge of gratitude flooded me – that she was, after all, free and alone. I felt drunk with remission. Her face was a foot from mine. Defencelessly, with a compulsion that had nothing to do with happiness, I stooped towards it – I had the sensation of falling through a black ocean – and found her mouth.

If I could stop Time, I'd stop it there. Yet the instant was touched too by an unaccountable recognition. It was as though the moment couldn't be my own, and that I had lived an instant from the life of somebody else. Someone unimaginable. The feeling didn't quite leave me. It was only suppressed by my vehemence for her mouth. Her lips lived their own life. They were elvishly mobile, turned upward at the corners to smile. To this day I don't know if they were so different from anybody else's (in the hospital they'd been scored by tiny, vertical lines, as if by a razor, and had lost their fullness.) But I kissed them on and on in a frenzy to taste and enter them, to pour my whole body in, far in, away.

I wish now I'd never said that banal "*I love you*", which rang alarm bells down all her mind's corridors (I've heard those bells myself, so I know.) But it fell from my lips automatically, like overripe fruit. I was drugged by confession. I barely noticed the faint furrows sprung up between her eyebrows.

We were a long time kissing. Once, with astonishment, I opened my eyes and saw that we were still standing by the stagnant pool, and that the sky was still light. And once, feeling the unbearable tightness of her breasts, I whispered: "Please, can't we? Please."

"Not now, not tonight."

Whenever she separated her body from mine I enveloped

her almost in panic: some deep disbelief in me could only be convinced by the touch of her.

But it's unbearable to write this now, to remember, after what happened. I'll return to that later. But not now. For the moment I want to stay here. Just for a while. I want to stay here. So leave me. *I want to stay here.*

Three

Back in the nineteenth century the asylum contained more than thirteen hundred inmates. Their beds and palliasses lined the wider corridors, and crowded into the courtyards under awnings whose iron brackets still project from the stone. Today the place accommodates four hundred, and the passages peter out in disused dormitories heaped with rusty bedsteads or laundry cases, and in smaller rooms sealed off altogether.

Nowadays they don't admit many new Chronics, and the average age of the patients is growing older with the building. The facilities for anything more energetic than walking have almost gone. In the gardens the vegetable plots once worked by the Acutes were grassed in years ago, and the badminton lines painted on the polished floors of the community hall have been rubbed faint by the passage of wheelchairs. As for the old football pitch, whose posts still stand in the field, its use is scarcely a memory.

The wards themselves have shrivelled but cheered up. Faraday is typical; it houses only eighteen patients. The jolly carpets and wallpapers surround this human dereliction like a forced smile. You'd think half these Acutes were already institutionalised. By late afternoon most of them are sitting round the walls staring at the television and tapping their cigarettes into the ashbins by each chair. A few read thrillers or comics, or play cards and Monopoly together in the dining area. Others lie sprawled in the dormitory, exhausted or drugged. There's no privacy. The dormitory beds leave only slivers of cubicles, narrower than Sunningrove's, each one containing a single wardrobe for all a man's possessions. The charge nurse sits in a glass office overlooking the TV-room on one side and the dormitory on the other. Nothing escapes him. He controls a dashboard of buzzers and emergency lights, and can speak by microphone to the farthest parts of the ward. The doors are all panelled in wired glass for spying through, and even the lavatories have two-way locks.

It's a miniature universe. Among the patients delicate hierarchies of power and dependence evolve. Certain armchairs become the privilege of certain men – the coveted ones are nearest the television – and tiny republics develop at mealtimes, depending on who is eating with whom. The giving of cigarettes or small change follows a subtle web of authority and obligation. After a patient has left for the outside, a furtive regrouping takes place, and the moment a new one arrives he finds his niche almost unconsciously in a social skein inherited through many permutations from years before. It's like a family; and its network lays a security over their personal isolations. They know their place.

Yet many seem unreachably sunk within themselves, so that their conversation may be less like understanding than an impersonal flashing of signals. They're drugged on Valium or Ativan these days – or Largactil if those don't work. But after a short spell on Largactil their limbs seize up, and their jaws sometimes can't swallow properly and stiffen into set grins. They're given pills to neutralise its side-effects, and then pills to neutralise the side-effects of the pills, until their bodies are a battleground for four or five different medications.

But the physical effects don't often show. Evans, who's scarcely more than a boy, walks as if he's being wrenched sideways and upwards, but I think it's hereditary. Otherwise there's only Sheldon, an elderly ex-miner who strokes the air with beautiful, disfigured hands exactly as if he were playing a violin. He can hardly hold a pen, but he wrote an evasively impersonal essay on 'The Most Important Time of my Life', recounting his youth down the pit.

'The Boss' is the bastard of the ward. I suppose there's always got to be one. He's in his late forties, and a depressive, I'd guess: grossly built, with rounded shoulders and a neck like a wrestler's. When I suggested he write out some part of his life-story, he just said: "Go fuck yourself, Pashley." He helps the kitchen porters wheeling in supplies, and sometimes earns as much as £70 a week. He never entrusts his money to the Nursing Officer, but leaves it protruding in fat wads from his jacket pocket. Then he'll hang the jacket on a nearby chair, and watch. If anybody approaches it, even one of the staff, he starts to cough meaningfully and his mutinous little eyes flicker between the person and the money as if to say 'I know what you're thinking.' He's surrounded himself by a circle of three or four card-playing cronies, who sit in the dining area most afternoons, gambling at poker, although it's officially forbidden. Most of the others are afraid of him; but if he's confronted by one of the charge nurses, he suddenly turns abject, his shoulders hunch and his lower lip falls forward showing rotted teeth which look too small for his mouth.

My favourite is old Gregory, who was a librarian in his previous life, as he calls it, and always dresses with quaint self-respect. He is thoughtful and rather academic. He reminds me of Nisbet: the same physical frailty, the same match-stick legs and arms and retractable-looking neck. He has a betraying mannerism – a perpetual, swift, flickering, snake-like washing of his hands, which he can only allay by lacing his fingers together. Most of the time he talks quite objectively, but he's been in and out of here for years. Now that I've gained his trust the eyes behind their glasses take on an odd, reticent sweetness. He keeps his whole past life stacked in his wardrobe – thick bundles of letters from his parents and sisters, all dead, family photographs going back to the twenties, and boxes full of mementoes decipherable only to himself: dried flowers and leaves, Victorian bookmarkers, coloured pebbles, four broken watches, a portrait miniature, a dried seahorse. Even as a boy, he said, he could never bear to throw away anything. He felt he would be losing hold of himself, his reality. At other times he says he's lost himself anyway and that he shouldn't have been born, that he was a mistake, his parents didn't want him. But he doesn't blame them, he always adds. He wouldn't have wanted himself either.

I often find him sipping tea with the Chronics in the social room. He feels safer there, away from anyone who will understand him, and it was years before I broke a little into his secrecy. Sometimes even now, while we're talking, he will suddenly shelter away from me, hugging himself tremulously, pathetically, with both hands clamped in his armpits. Recently I asked him about Sophia but he'd never talked to the female patients, he said, and he hadn't seen anybody who answered to my description. "If I were you I'd try to speak to Administration," he said. "They've got us all on file. Administration will tell you anything you want to know."

But I wasn't sure what I wanted to know. Patients' diagnoses are kept strictly secret. For the next four days I found it impossible to concentrate on teaching in the ward. Every few minutes I'd be staring through the window into the gardens, following the path from the bench to the side-entrance and back again to the bench. But the only woman I saw there was an elderly Chronic cradling a thermos. She remained all afternoon, while I silently fumed at her as if she were ousting Sophia. Several times I went and sat there myself, as if this would magically draw Sophia, and looked again across the sward of crocuses, dying now, to where daffodils were appearing in the old football field. I began to feel the thing had been a dream.

I haunted the community hall and the social room. It was futile talking to the older female Chronics – they only made deprecatory murmurs or didn't answer – and the nursing staff I questioned all served on men's wards. For a while I loitered outside the iron door with the curtained panel, but nobody came in or went out. It seemed as impenetrable as a harem. I came to loathe the sight of it.

The only female Chronic who was even middle-aged, sitting one afternoon in a corner of the community hall, was suffering from some kind of glandular disorder: enormously fat and stuffing her mouth with sweets. I held almost no hope as I sat

44

beside her. I said: "Can you tell me, is there a Sophia Brown in your ward?"

"There are all sorts of wards." She gave me a sweet. "You want to know how many? Many."

"And which are you in?"

"Nightingale. Nightingale B."

I couldn't tell how far gone she was. Her manner was harsh, off-hand. "Do you know a Sophia Brown?"

"Sophia." She gazed at the ceiling, her mouth open, gums black with liquorice. "There are many Sophias. You want to know how many? Many."

"Sophia Brown."

"I know Sophia Brown."

"When did she come?"

"She's always coming. Telling the funniest stories. Ha-ha-ha-haaah . . . D'you know the one about Sophia Brown? Oh my dear Lord . . ."

I tried to choke down my wretchedness, sense of contamination. I didn't want to go on. But I demanded fiercely: "Do you know Sophia Brown? Is she in your ward?"

"Brown. There are many Browns." She blew into the liquorice bag. "You know how many? Many."

After this I wrote Sophia a letter and posted it in the hospital mail-box; I gave a date and time for meeting her at Inner Reception, which is the farthest patients can go. But she didn't reply, and she didn't come. Soon afterwards I discovered that the women's wards were being offered an outing to Raglan. I watched almost forty embark on the coach at the main entrance; but she wasn't among them.

My mind raged with feasible or foolish possibilities – that she'd escaped the hospital in order to evade me, that she'd been a short-term Acute and had gone away. I even entertained the macabre possibility that she was, in fact, a perfectly sane visiting doctor, but had feigned madness in order to revenge herself on me.

These thoughts only faded late at night. Then I'd simply remember her new face and hands and voice, and fall into a confusion of dreams. Waking early, and deeply depressed, I'd wonder what I was doing trying to see her anyway. Better to let her be. I felt utterly bereft. Even if I knew her clinical diagnosis, what could I ever do? It's only in legends that love retrieves people from the dead.

A new patient arrived at Faraday. You could tell he was different the moment he burst into the ward. Most newcomers come in furtively, and slither round the walls to find an inconspicuous chair, or by-pass the other inmates with their eyes averted in hanging heads. But this time the door flew open on a pudgy young man with florid cheeks and a halo of brilliant yellow hair. He gazed round the ward with soft grey eyes and a soft smile and his arms extended as if he'd been crucified against the door. He said: "I love you, I love you all."

The room was full. The Boss and his clique were hunched in one corner, thumbing their decks of cards, Gregory and I sitting in another, and the rest of them scattered about the armchairs waiting for lunch. Nobody said a word. Then the man uncrucified himself and danced into the middle of the room. He was dressed in skin-tight jeans and a primrose-yellow bomber jacket. "It's good to be here, it's good to be among you!"

"Holy hell." The Boss burped. "A real, live, goddam, sixties flower-fucker."

But the man went round us all shaking our hands, clasping them in both his and saying: "I'm Tom Orgill. Tom. Everything's going to be all right."

"Like shit it is," said the Boss. "Where've you sprung from? A pansy-bed?"

Orgill scooped up one of the Boss's great spatular hands and pumped it. "I'm no gay, mister. Here's betting I've had more women than you've had farts. It's a beautiful world! Good to know you, mister. Good to know you!"

The Boss pulled his hand back. But Orgill's soft, pink fingers were enclosing Sheldon's now, interrupting the noiseless violin sonata. "That's a beautiful sound you've got there! Beautiful! I'm Tom Orgill. . . ." He rushed on to Gregory's hands, which were writhing miserably. "Everything's going to be all right!"

"Let us hope so, yes," said Gregory.

"I'm Pashley," I said. "I teach English here."

His hands were moist and hot, like sponge puddings. "Glad to see you, Mr Pashley. Glad! English. Marvellous! I love language. Do you love language? 'For, lo, the winter is past, the rain is over and gone; the time of the singing of birds is come . . .' What's on the agenda?" His whole body was weaving and dancing in front of me, bursting with an unbearable self-generated excitement.

"We've got an essay competition going," I said, but suddenly it sounded lame. "The Most Important Time of My . . ."

"Great! I love essays and poetry. Does anyone here like poetry?" His eyes darted round the others, but found a strange confusion there. Some of them had twisted their heads away or were staring down at the hands he'd shaken, as if he might have left something behind. Others were observing him with a vague, wan hopefulness, like children watching for the postman.

"I *love* poetry." It was the wrenched-up youth Evans. He talked in a fluting whisper. "Sometimes . . . sometimes I try writing it. It's no good of course. But sometimes . . ."

"Soul-mate!" Orgill leapt across and embraced him, lifting him half out of his chair. "I'm composing poetry all the time. Reams of it! All the time! Look here. You and me – we'll get together."

"Blimey," said the Boss.

Orgill swivelled round and spread out his arms to the ward again. "We're all in this together, aren't we? If we don't help one another, where're we going to be? Everything's going to be all right, I tell you."

Evans fluted: "That's what I always said."

That afternoon, in Occupational Therapy, Orgill was everywhere. The motherly therapist kept saying: "Mr Orgill, would you please sit down . . . you're distracting the other patients, Mr Orgill . . . *please*, Mr Orgill. . . ." The Faraday therapy room is long, like a gallery, and it's hung with the

47

work of the patients – mostly paintings of people and domestic pets. Many of these are unconscious studies in alienation. The men are brutal, the women hard; the cats bristle and leer like tigers; the dogs have crocodile jaws. One end of the gallery is cleared for simple gymnastic exercises, the other monopolised by the long arts table, piled with crayons, paints and modelling clay.

It stimulated Orgill to fever pitch. He started a seascape in watercolours, tried to shape a plasticene horse, gave this up and flung himself into drawing nude bathers.

"Mr Orgill, would you please. . . ."

"I'm just going to help Mr Evans."

Evans fidgeted and smiled. He was creating a collage landscape with scraps of cloth and string and autumn leaves. It was dense and strange. The sky exploded in violent purples and gashes of orange, and the ground beneath it was a suppurating pool of fallen leaves.

"Wow!" Orgill stared. "How about *that*!"

Evans glanced up at him. "Do you really like it?"

"*Like* it? It's better'n a *Picasso*, I tell you! Here, boys, have you seen what Evans has been doing?" He lifted the picture above his head. "Look! If any of you can beat *that* I'll shell out a fiver."

Evans blushed and writhed smiling on his seat. "It's not that great."

"It *is* that great." Orgill settled down with him to speckle the leaves with tiny birds cut out of black felt. "You could make a living out of things like this. You've got a natural colour sense, 'course you have."

For five minutes the room was quiet. Almost all you could hear were the grunts and gasps of a small, square-built man who was lifting dumb-bells in the gymn section. He wore shorts and a T-shirt today, but usually went about half undressed, with a badly-knotted tie tucked into his trousers and sticking out between his half-open flies. The others called him Prick.

For a minute or two Orgill's eyes flickered back and forth, then he jumped up and bounded over to try weightlifting.

("*Please*, Mr Orgill, would you be still for *one* minute.") He jerked and sweated with a small dumb-bell in each hand, his high-coloured cheeks turned scarlet and his lips a pursed-up bud of whistling breath. Prick watched him without expression – I never saw Prick with an expression – then handed him a big, single dumb-bell. "You try? You can, huh? Try that one then."

Orgill grasped it with fervour, jerked it to shoulder-height then tried to press it higher. His arms quivered and the veins started from his soft-looking wrists. Prick watched. The Boss, doing nothing, watched too. Orgill's face became a crimson grimace around his clenched teeth. His neck swelled and pulsed. His hair was a shaking mass of light. Then, with a little cry, he straightened his arms and held the thing aloft.

"Not bad," said Prick. "You're stronger'n you look."

Orgill breathed "Yeah", but looked drained. When he returned and noticed me at the table he muttered "Ah, the essay," and hunted about dazedly until the therapist found him a note-pad. Then he started writing in a fierce, jagged hand, more and more rapidly, peeling the finished pages from the pad. He was trembling slightly. I guessed they'd put him on Largactil.

"You all right?" Gregory was sitting beside him.

"Yeah. Bit puffed, that's all." He fingered the discarded pages. "What're you doing there?"

Gregory was modelling the head of a woman in red clay. He'd been doing this for weeks, gently, ruminatively, hollowing out her starved cheeks and eye-sockets and bitter indentations round the nose. He touched her face with only the tips of his fingers. It seemed more an act of meditation than of sculpture. I think he'd really finished it weeks back, but he could never release his pieces, let them be finally created, and in a day or two, I guessed, he'd start to break the portrait down (if it was a portrait), nagging at the clay until the face would seem diseased, almost a skull, and he'd say: "It wasn't right, not a real likeness. . . ."

Orgill stared at the head. He was starting to revive. He said: "She's not very pretty, is she?"

49

"No : . . no. Not very." Gregory inched away from him in his chair. His fingers trembled over her.

Orgill said: "You should tilt the nose up, that'd be better. Give her a retroussé."

"She's meant to be like this."

"You know, I hate to say this," Orgill said, "but I don't agree with that head. Why create something so . . . I'm sorry but it's *ugly*. Works of art should be beautiful. Beautiful!"

Gregory swallowed. "I expect so, yes . . . I'm sure you're right." His eyes were blinking rapidly, continuously, behind their glasses. "But well . . . she's just *there*, you see. . . ."

Orgill's hands were on the table now, itching. "I'd say she needs a bit of flesh on her."

"No."

But the soft, sponge-pudding hands came crawling over, kneading a chunk of fallen clay. They lifted to the face.

"No!"

"Mr Orgill!" The therapist was sighing. "Please don't touch the patient's work. He knows what he's doing." Orgill's hands regrouped on his lap. The therapist went on: "Now will anyone who feels like it join in our weekly discussion? Last time, if you remember, we talked about our favourite animals. This week I want to ask you what you'd do if you won the football pools." She beamed round at everybody.

These discussions, I think, are intended to activate and concentrate the mind. But nobody volunteered a word. A few patients dithered with their artwork, then stopped, crestfallen. Only Gregory went on tentatively, automatically, eroding the woman's face with his fingertips. The wheezing and snorting of Prick under his dumb-bells died away, and he came and stared at us, his hair all spikes and sweat.

"Well then," the therapist began, "We'll start with Mr Sheldon. What would you do with the money, Mr Sheldon?"

Sheldon started playing his violin, stared at the floor, said nothing. Her gaze travelled round the table with a look of kindly disappointment. Evans crammed his fingers into his mouth. Prick said: "I dunno. I just dunno."

Gregory momentarily abandoned the head and took off his

glasses. His hands began their serpent-like washing. "It's a very hard question. There are so many things, too many . . . Far, far too many . . . I'm so sorry . . ." and his voice petered out.

Then the Boss, with indecipherable courtesy, said: "If I had the money, ma'am, I'd purchase our sculptor here some hand soap, and Mr Sheldon a violin."

The therapist pursed her lips, nonplussed, unable to decode his tone. "That would be very kind . . . and Mr Orgill?"

"Me! I know what I'd do! How's this for an idea, boys? I'd start a *centre*, a meeting-place. It'd be a centre for the opening up of awareness. Yes, for releasing the wonder, the beauty! It'd be . . ."

But suddenly I wasn't hearing his voice any more. Another voice, much softer, had intruded and overlaid it. For a second I thought it was in my head, it was so deeply remembered, so wanted, and I looked around a little dazed. Then I realised that the voice penetrated here, into the room, muffled but perfectly recognisable, and that it came from beyond the thin partition wall behind my back, in wordless tones and cadences.

I got up and went softly out of the gallery. The passage was empty. The adjoining room was labelled 'O.T. Sewing.' When I put my ear to the door I could hear the whirr and thump of Singer treadles inside, and faint voices. I inched it open. The room was very small. Heaps of faded dresses and curtain-covers strewed the floor, and four women were tapping and clicking at the machines in disconnected murmurs of conversation. Sophia was seated staring straight at me, less than four feet away.

"What are you doing here?" she said.

"I heard your voice."

"Oh yes. It's very distinctive. Very distinctive."

My heart jumped. Her eyes had lost some of the fixity of before. They flickered vaguely back and forth. She must have had a change of drug, I thought. Sometimes they met mine, veered away, came back. The muted light in the room made her look younger.

I crouched among the pile of clothes beside her table. Two

of the other women hadn't even noticed me. The third had her back turned; her head was bandaged, and tufts of grey hair sprouted between the strips. Sophia was mending the seams on one of those shapeless, jumble-sale dresses.

I said softly: "How long have you been in this hospital?"

"I've always been here." She looked faintly distressed, tapped at her cheeks with her fingers. "Can you see me?"

"You're *not* transparent."

She looked as if she might return to her stitching, but didn't, murmured: "Good."

The woman with the bandaged head said: "The therapist'll be back."

Once Sophia's stare held mine, then she smiled. At such moments, although at heart I knew it was myth, I imagined her suddenly focusing into herself again. But what precisely was now herself, I didn't know. Was it still there? Or had it died? She asked again: "What are you doing here?"

I said very slowly, precisely: "I'm a volunteer teacher. I'm here in school holidays."

Vaguely: "Often? Like Miss Kedward?"

"Who's she?"

"The O.T. The Occupational. She does things."

The bandaged woman said: "She'll be coming back."

"Yes, like Miss Kedward. But I teach English."

"English?"

"Words, essays." Almost hopelessly I added: "Sophia, write one about your life – the important time." I had a fleeting mirage of her remembering, of her recovering herself through memory. "Will you write it?" I took her hand. "The important time."

"Daniel, she's coming back."

To hear her say my name brought a ridiculous thrill. I made her repeat it. "Daniel."

"Daniel."

I said: "I'll help you write. We'll remember together."

"I remember alone." Her gaze wandered to our hands.

"*Do* you remember?"

"She's coming back." Softly at first, diffidently, then with a

52

hot, firm pressure, she was squeezing my hand. The response of this flesh to mine was almost unbearable. I simply crouched there, searching her face. But when she smiled again it was just pretty, meaningless, it might have been directed at a landscape or a memory (perhaps it was).

Her mannerisms now were barely those I remembered at all. They were all transmuted: blunter, vaguer. I had to learn new facial expressions, find out what they meant, if anything; but every time I adapted to one of these shadows I was afraid I was losing its original. I was afraid I was starting to forget what she'd once been like.

The bandaged woman turned in her chair. She was clasping a soft toy against her bosom; she'd been stitching it together. "She's coming back." Sophia's eyes darted at the door.

I said: "Where can we meet?"

"I come here. I'm always here."

Stupidly I believed her. "Sophia. Tell me. What is my name?"

"Daniel." Her hand deserted mine.

"What's your name?"

"You said Sophia."

"You *are* Sophia."

"Sophia," she said. She seemed to be trying it out. "Yes. But she's coming back. We have high tea now." She giggled (another unfamiliar habit). "It's disgusting."

I got up. "I'll see you tomorrow." I looked at her until she looked back at me. "I'm Daniel, you're Sophia. Remember."

She stooped to pick up a dress.

A few minutes later I was back on Faraday ward. The patients were lining up to receive their drugs. Obscurely, I felt I'd made an advance, but exactly to what point I could advance, I didn't know. I'd asked some of the nurses about the prognosis for Chronics, and they said they had never known one cured. Living in the limbo of one another's insanity, they simply deteriorated, slipped away.

Orgill was saying: "Christ! Why am I on Largactil? That's heavy, isn't it?"

"That's what's been prescribed," the staff nurse said.

Orgill stared at the pills, seven white capsules mounded in his palm. "Well I hope they know their shop, these doctors, 'cos I'm a free individual. Free! Every man has a right to decide what penetrates his body. And every woman too." He pinched her chin. "What happens if I just *pretend* to swallow these little bleeders?"

"They'd be prescribed to you in syrup form," the nurse said. "Then we can be sure." She flirted with her eyes, but didn't go until he'd swallowed.

"I claim the right to snuck away the next lot of pellets behind my teeth," Orgill announced to the ward, "and spit them out for whoever wants."

The Boss had settled to playing cards with Prick. "You think they wouldn't know, huh?" He jabbed a thumb at the blank television screen. "D'you imagine *that thing*'s there just to give you the jollies? They're watching us now. That's the eye."

Orgill squinted at it. He couldn't know, yet, that the Boss was paranoid. "Whose eye?"

"*The* eye, you simp. You make a king looney of yourself, Orgill, and I'll tell you what they'll do. One of those sweet little nurses, she'll run up behind you with a needle and fill your arse with intravenous Valium. Yup. You'll be out mute as a flounder in ten seconds. Then you'll wake up in Disturbed ward with a knitting-circle of Chronics. That'll cure you of your freedom crap." He was enjoying himself. His cheeks and chin bunched into shining white cannonballs whenever he smiled his meaningless smile. "And if you go on being beef-witted, Orgill, know what they'll do? They'll put you on electro-convulsive until you don't know whether you're Arthur or Martha. When you come out your eyes'll just be burnt-out piss-holes."

"Are you bollocking me, Boss? You're bollocking me." But Orgill didn't look happy. He touched my arm and muttered: "What's wrong with that guy? How long has he been in?" Then he thrust his essay papers at me. "You show that around, Prof. That'll cheer the boys. What they need in this place is celebration." His face ignited, as if he'd turned a switch. "Someone to show them what it's about, show them the glory!"

I took his few pages into the dormitory. Their handwriting started angular but steady, then it declined into a fierce scrawl that joined half the words together and leapt off the edge of the last page as if it had forgotten to come back. I read:

This whole idea blows my mind because whole days and even individual minutes come at me like they're so important they obliterate all the other times and I wonder why people still recognise me, I feel so changed. That's how it is. Like everything's on fire out there without burning, or some kind of planet wheeling across your eyes and you just lying there ogling it. Yes it comes from out there like that, so that sometimes I just get dizzy and want to close my eyes from the phosphorescence.

But sure there was an important time, more important than all the other important times – the day my sister Margery takes me to the theatre because she's got a friend in the chorus and two free tickets. It was some sort of kids' panto, but beautiful, like there was nothing in the world but this throbbing furnace of music and laughter, and I sitting in the darkness there gazing at this girl. She's dressed as a dragonfly or something, but anyone can tell she's a girl. Her boobs are sticking out under her wings better'n angels' and she has a mouth like a prize mulberry. I says to Margery who's your friend? and she points right at this dragonfly. And afterwards we go backstage into the chorus changing-rooms and there's all these angels and dragonflies, yards of them, taking off their wigs and wings and knickers and getting into jeans to go back home, and Julie glowing like the Koh-i-noor in the middle.

Sixty seconds later I'd asked her out and a day after that we're lying together like we've never known anybody else. She was pure woman, soft and downy with tits as big as wine-corks and a whole little nectar-pot between her thighs. She could even sing. I went kind of crazy. For weeks we'd be up all night and when I got to work at the post office I'd drop asleep over the old ladies' pension books and they'd think I'd kicked it for good. Yes I wanted to marry Julie. She loved things. She turned the whole world so it was like walking inside a diamond, and I knew then love wasn't blind at all, love opens your eyes and polishes them clean.

Still I don't know why she left me. But she said it was too much, I'd burnt her through and through, like she was an ironing-board. I thought she despised my job, but it's an okay job, I tell her, it's not just counting stamps, I do motor licence forms and I meet people all the time, marvellous people. But still she leaves me. You need help, she says.

Then I go right down, I can't say how far down. But deep enough so I end up with this analyst. He's two foot nothing and smells of dead cabbages. His face is just a soup-plate, not a proper face at all, so that I felt it didn't count when I smashed it in. For half an hour I tell him how I feel and he sits there like he's just a pair of specs above a scribbling-pad. I tell him Julie's rejected love, rejected the glory, she can't stand the blaze, because that's what she said herself. I tell him that.

At last a crack opens in the soup-plate and it speaks: "We find 'love' a rather misused term in my profession," he pules, "we try to be more specific. I have your medical reports here" – and he waves them like they was a wand – "and to be frank, you've already received a preliminary diagnosis of hypomania . . ." and so on. Jesus! I tell you for a minute I couldn't see the man for tears of rage or I'd have hit him earlier. I'd always thought these shrinks flattened you on a couch, but he'd put me in an armchair and was sitting opposite me propped up like the Pope.

"I love her," I said. "I love her."

So he gets worried and starts to throw science at me. "Mr Orgill," he says in a voice like a tap squeaking, "your diagnosis suggests an overactive limbic system . . ." But I can't even write how he went on, he got so inhuman. My whole love, all the light and heat and wonder of it, all the laughter and the soft-breathed words were snuffed out on his scribbling-pad. I was psy-this and schiz-that and this-otic and that-oid.

Then I whopped him. And I'm stronger than I look, as you've seen. The poor little bugger just dropped over backwards like a drunk and lay doggo. And I bellowed in his ear: "I *love* her, I *love* her, I *love* her!"

I know I shouldn't have done it, I know, and for a minute I was shit-scared because I thought I'd killed him. But soon afterwards, of course, he was ringing the police.

That's why I'm here. But I tell you it was a kind of righteousness made me do it. I meant to open his eyes instead of blacking them, make him see the real stars and tell him I –

But this last sentence skipped off the page and didn't come back; and Orgill forgot to ask me what I thought of his piece, but carried it round the ward saying: "Who wants to see my essay? Anybody want a read?"

A middle-aged man they called Buddha (because he was fat and meditated) seized on it as if it were holy writ. He had taken to shadowing Orgill and collecting his litter of half-smoked cigarette butts.

Orgill stared out of the window at the reddening sunset, while Gregory squirmed away from him along the wall, until he was standing beside me. "I don't think I could read it . . . or perhaps later. I think these things should be private. You won't show mine to the ward, you promised?" But he chose this time to hand it to me. "It's nothing I can be proud of, nothing at all."

Orgill said: "How's that for a sunset, fellows?" Around his silhouette in the window, the sky was in flames. "Look at that and believe anything!"

It was odd, I suppose, but nobody had noticed the sunsets from here before. It was as if sunsets didn't happen once you were inside.

The Boss looked up. "Don't come on all mystical, Orgill, for Chrissake. That, if you want to know, is a ball of helium being interfered with by the earth going round. I've done my science. And the gaudy pink you remark on is due. . . ." But his voice grumbled out, because he couldn't remember.

Gregory glanced nervously between him and Orgill then back to his essay in my hands. I thought he'd ask for it back in a minute, so I walked off into the dormitory, but he followed me. "You won't show it to the others, will you, you said you wouldn't? Perhaps to the psychiatrist, if it can help. But I don't see how. You see, I don't know how real it is. I'm always thinking something, and then I start to doubt and think the opposite, and in the end there's nothing left. . . ."

He put out his hand to take back the essay, then shook his head and disclaimed it with a little pushing gesture.

It was written meticulously in a backward-sloping hand on ten or eleven sheets of letter-writing paper. Its o's and y's and g's were tightly knotted or elaborately looped, and numberless words had been neatly crossed out and made illegible, then superscribed with corrections:

The most important time of my life, I am told, happened even before I was born when I caused my mother yet another disfiguring and painful pregnancy. I was a 'mistake' in any case, she said, I'd been conceived when she and my father were just making up for a tiff in each other's arms. My father always said she and I looked at each other through opposite ends of a telescope, as it were. I saw her too big and she saw me too small.

For me, then, the most important time was his death. It was only then that I became a grown-up, although I can't say I've ever felt this state properly, no I can't say that. But when he died I was already sixteen years old, and to be sixteen in those far-off days of pit closures and industrial migrations was already to be a man. It was from this time, I think, that some inner distress started taking hold of me, although even now it isn't clear to me. Those were the bad times, of course. The post-war prosperity for coal and iron had gone, and South Wales became a kind of wilderness, all the young migrated to the Midlands and the old just wasting away. There were quarter of a million unemployed, more than thirty per cent of us, and families close to starvation. My father was a foreman in the Dowlais steelworks, and we were better off than most. But they closed in 1930, and he never recovered. He was forty-two, and at that age he didn't stand a hope. Even to be twenty-five and unemployed was to be nearly finished.

58

That's the time I remember him. He was like me, sensitive and too thin, but much more intelligent, very intelligent, and wonderful on the piano. Yet he was condemned to spend his days in the unemployeds' club, playing dominoes. I think he couldn't face my mother, no I think not. He was already greying fast at the temples and his face was greyer still. In the evenings, at first, I recall him playing Welsh folk songs and smoking a churchwarden pipe and saying the good days would come back, that the Belgians would be put out of the steel business and we'd recover the markets lost to the States while we were suffering on the Somme. But even as a boy I sensed he was 'blowing bubbles', as my mother called it, and eventually the churchwarden pipe broke and wasn't replaced, and the piano went silent and my sisters were sent away into service in London. For a while my father worked on a hillside allotment and tried to join the Land Resettlement scheme, but I watched our meals go from scrag of mutton to cabbage and potato broth, until the margarine was spread so thin I didn't even notice when it vanished.

But my mind, in those days, was full of other things. I belonged to a group which studied the Gospels and Revelation most evenings. Methodism wasn't melodramatic any more, of course, the fervent revivalist years were over. People were even saying the chapels' days were numbered, and we felt embattled as we gathered in the prayer-hall in our blue serge suits under the dour pastor's son. But the fires of Hell hounded us all, me more than any of them. Sometimes I was filled with a sublime humility and a consciousness of my sin. But the pastor's son would ask us to confess our trespasses out loud in earnest of our prostration before Almighty God. Then I would try to forget my sins, the embarrassing ones, and I'd just confess the easy ones, and he'd commend me for my honest confession, and the rest would add "Amen" and "Aye-aye". But later I'd remember the other things I'd thought and done, things in the night, and I'd fall on my knees and ask God and the Holy Saviour to forgive and preserve me from the Gnashing and the Wrath to come, and I'd start to weep.

To this day I don't know what my father died of. My

mother said he just gave up, and I think you can die of that, yes I do. I saw him fold himself away, as it were. His cheeks grew scooped and sallow. But the thing is, he no longer believed. Soon before he went he said to me, but gently: "What's all this Bible study then, Gregory?"

"I want to be a pastor," I said, but I don't know why I said it. I didn't know what I wanted. Always, when I thought I wanted something, I wondered why it was that thing and not some other thing, and then I'd get confused and want the other thing, and finally nothing at all. It's difficult.

My father said: "You're too good for the chapel, boy. We've managed you an education. Try the schools."

"I want God," I said. I was only a boy, although sixteen.

Then, I remember, my father reached out from his chair and drew me against him, against his body's awful thinness under the blue jacket, and said: "But it's no good staying here in the south, boy, the chapels are emptying, don't you see, they've no funds. God needs money, just like you will. He's gone to the Midlands, boy. We've got nearly forty per cent unemployment. You'll find God in Birmingham now."

Within a month father was dead, but I was still listening to him, have listened to him since. He'd been a paragon of Methodist virtue, of temperance and thrift and industry, he'd believed in equality before God and the holiness of the individual. But God had closed down the Dowlais steelworks in 1930 and he was out of a job from then until his death. The double line of friends who preceded his hearse in the rain were all the same. They hadn't an overcoat between them.

It was from this time that I became a 'distressed area', like my town. For a while I went on going to the Bible study group, but I couldn't concentrate because my father was in Hell fire. If Dowlais hadn't closed, I thought, he'd be in heaven, and I knew something was badly wrong, and that a just god didn't commit things like that. I began to ask questions, but the others were too clever for me. There were replies to everything, about man's free-will, God's inscrutability and so forth, and they wondered why I was questioning, and they smelt my fading faith. But I didn't want to hate God, not to hate Him, so I started hating the dour pastor's son instead, and I let God off by deciding He did not exist. And all at once I started to look at the Bible group differently, just as if I was outside a house I'd once been inside, and suddenly I could see what I'd never seen before, that it's architecture was decadent and it didn't fit in properly with the street it stood in, the street of my experience. I noticed that the shape of all their faces was different from the shape of my face. Theirs were square, so to speak, and mine was triangular. It did seem strange. After this discovery about our different faces, I only went on going because I liked a girl called Bridget, who was devout. We were often asked to improvise prayers in turn, and my prayer would usually ask intercession for nurses, because she was a trainee nurse. But Bridget always spoke the same prayer, which went something like: "Blessed Holy Spirit, bring me ever closer to the Lord Jesus, I pray, for He is my life. I pray bring me closer to *Him*, ever closer to *Him*, to *Him*," and she'd rock up and down in her chair with her head buried in her hands, and I'd suddenly think how her Emlyn had left her for the Midlands, and that the Lord Jesus was just standing in.

It was then that I left. But my mother wanted me for a preacher and she didn't let me forget, and I know I've cut myself off from all forgiveness if I'm wrong. The ways of God must be mysterious because the ways of men are mysterious. We're all frightening. In Revelation it says that those not written in the book of life will be cast into a lake of fire. I just don't know. But I left and went to Swansea, and I never picked up a Bible again.

Like that I laid my father to rest.

Four

Last night I dreamt that my head was split up into twenty different rooms and that in each one Sophia was sitting, quite still, usually in a corner, reading or staring directly ahead of her. Even now, awake, I feel as if she'd always been there, and that our first meeting was simply recognition. In the dream her face was that of ten years ago – the same face that I had so frenziedly tried to discover and assimilate, and had failed.

The impact of those days has nothing to do with their number. I saw her for barely a month. About twice a week we'd have supper together, and on weekends walk along the canals of the Usk or over the Black Mountains. The lambs and ravens of Brecon still make a noise in my memory. Once we went to the theatre in Bristol, she radiant in a white evening dress for which she kept apologising ("Christ, I look old-fashioned"); and once to the coast where we swam in a cold sea and shivered in each other's arms.

Then we'd lie together on the sofa in her sittingroom, or among cushions on its floor, kissing and fondling with the passion of teenagers. A whole evening passed simply in my exploration of her face as it laughed at me from the cushions. And even this was like trying to map a continent. No sooner had my kisses exhausted her eyes or lips, than her neck or ears or her cheekbones' aloofness drew me as if I'd never touched them before, and my lips would travel intoxicated round her hairline's softness to find the furrow of her nape. Then I would stare into her blue gaze and try to dissect its power. I examined where the irises lightened around the enlarged pupils, and saw how they intensified towards their rims into an azure brilliance. I scrutinised her black eyelashes and watched the narrowing of the lids when she smiled. Then I extinguished these eyes in kisses, until at last I thought: now I've compassed them, I've exorcised them. But the next moment, made strange by some new mood in her, they would be violently resurrected, watching me as if for the first time. With every change in her expression she became unknown again. Loving her was a long, delirious ache. Again and again, hour after hour, my mouth returned convulsively to seal her own, multiplied kisses on its velvet surrounding skin, ran my lips along the insides of hers, entered their darkness.

But sometimes then I'd feel a vague fear as my tongue swept in the void of that mouth, not answered by her own tongue but only by the mouth's slightly bitter-tasting walls: as if this were the beginning of nothingness. Yet I was weak with longing.

I thought about her so intensively that I stopped being sure of anything to do with her. I could no longer even tell if she were objectively beautiful. I longed to meet somebody who knew her, simply so I might ask them about her, just as if she were a stranger.

She only came to Sunningrove once. I can't explain this, but her presence destroyed it. The place splintered and withered about us wherever we walked. It lost all meaning. Nisbet sat with us for half an hour in my room, sipping sherry. He addressed her with old-world courtesy, which I enjoyed and she found ridiculous, and I wondered, watching him, if he were not secretly dazzled by her. But it was not until a long time afterwards that I found him alone; I didn't want to embarrass him with questions – and he never said.

When Sophia and I emerged from my rooms that night we ran into McQuitty in the staff corridor. I was glad. She was radiant on my arm. And he looked awkward and boorish. He seemed to have dwindled. He said: "So this is Juliet?"

But the sarcasm sounded embarrassed, and I realised that I'd never noticed him speak with a young woman. He did not offer her his hand. "Going home now are we? . . . Nearly twelve o'clock. . . ." while his fists pounded nervously at his sides, "Just as well . . . Pashley's got to coach the cricket eleven tomorrow. . . ." He pressed back against the passageway to let us pass.

It was only in the privacy of her cottage that my searching of her grew more urgent, but gentle. Even those long summer evenings were too short. She would often dress a little forbiddingly: in tight trousers and shirt. I wondered if this were a mute message to me. I unbuttoned these shirts surreptitiously, while I kissed her. The chance of her refusal haunted me. For another whole evening my fingers caressed the glossy warmth of her shoulders between her half-open blouse, squeezed their changing ligaments, eased away the collar to kiss them. One by one the delicate bastions of this body were falling. And a few days afterwards, as she lay on the floor in a summer dress, the tawny ovals of her calves slipped luxuriously into my hands; and at last, gently, I crept up and held all the satin strength of her thighs until my fingertips swarmed against her groin, up against the last soft flesh of her. But she laughed and squirmed away from me. And all the time, while her body trembled through my hands, my eyes would be tethered to hers: their chiaroscuro of wintry power and strange, intent compassion. Her eyes, I think, never closed. Even in the deepest kiss I would open mine to see hers staring at me, as if she were deciding what to do.

Sometimes I pleaded to enter her. But she always looked distracted, murmured about contraception or her period. Neither of us believed these. And at other times she simply asked me to wait. She never gave reasons. And I'd think: *Christ, I'm thirty-one.* But I could barely speak for love.

Yet now and again, when my mouth had smothered hers for the hundredth time or my caressing kindled her, her head would twist from side to side in its tumult of hair and she would let out little sharp cries of self-fear, and gasp and stare back at me with alarm. I cherished these moments. Usually when I whispered my love for her she would only smile; but at these times she breathed out "Darling, darling", and tilted back her flailing head for me to kiss her throat, and her mouth glistened with bared teeth.

There came a time when we lay almost naked together. Against her brown skin the bra's whiteness and the firmness beneath it became unendurable. When I peeled away this last protection and her breasts came fluttering into my hands, I felt a moment of possession more complete and delirious than ever happened again, pressing them against my mouth and eyes. "They're too small," she murmured, "much too small." This sudden shyness took me aback. I whispered: "No". As my lips opened against them her head began its twisting and disconnected cries. Then I knelt above her and drew those slender, sinuous, immaculate hands towards my penis, and we remained like this, ecstatically separate, her nipples erect at my touch, my erection tumultuous in her fingertips, holding each other by the nerve-ends of our bodies.

But it brought with it a kind of terror. Sometimes I had the sensation that we were holding each other on an abyss-edge. Everything was precarious, as if all this sweetness and ache created something black, precipitous, just beyond itself, so that I closed my eyes. But I supposed it was only a feeling.

Perhaps she needed to hold this last power over me. I don't know. Even in my dreams she held me yearning in her fingertips, yoked to her gaze, impotent. I couldn't even imagine a post-coital indifference to her body. That would have been release.

Those few weeks seem like years now. But it was only three times in all that we lay together quite like that. Then – I can't describe this – I sank into delirium with her, and slowly lost myself. My frustration disintegrated into a prolonged oblivion. My kisses slipped from her mouth and eyes down to the drugging softness of her breasts, her stomach. I would crush

65

her body to my face. I stopped having any idea what was going on in me. Or her. Or anywhere.

In July her mother had a cancer operation, and Sophia went away to nurse her, leaving me in wilderness. Everything around me had simply paled away and lost its substance. I tried to reconnect, but it was like emerging from a long hallucination. I couldn't find reality. If I'd kicked at furniture or walls, they'd have floated off like balloons. I'm sure the days became visually opaque, even when the sky was blue. Sophia had carried away the point of things. Whenever I imagined her, even at her mother's bedside, she inhabited brilliant light. Everything partook of life in proportion to its nearness to her. But as for me, I felt bodiless. The only objects around me which had presence were those she'd given me. I'd never been able to throw away anything she'd touched. I even had a fallen hairpin and the top of a soup carton from a take-away restaurant. These things now blazed in the unreality. They were my surety that she existed. Yet they were unbearable. And I couldn't put them away.

I knew the class curriculum so well that I could have taught with half my mind. Even so, I made mistakes. The boys started to take advantage of me. I sometimes caught my own voice stumbling and going vague. Once, while I was supervising prep, I heard a grinding rumble, and looked up to see the whole class still seated at its desks, grinning, but surging slowly, inexplicably, towards me. I jumped to my feet in horror, only to find that they'd improvised rollers under the bars of their desks and had advanced a mere foot in a gale of laughter. But I was sweating.

At first I spent the evenings in my room, waiting for her to telephone. She didn't. And I didn't ring her. I told myself I mustn't disturb her, but in fact I felt afraid: afraid to hear her voice indifferent to me. I was running away, I know, I even wondered if Charles were with her. I sensed she still saw him, but I never asked.

I began taking night walks along the roadside, trying to tire myself out. But I went like a somnambulist. The night turned everything intangible. A creeping paralysis of ivy muffled the ash tree silhouettes. The oaks were merely perforated cardboard against the summer sky. Sometimes I passed uncurtained windows shining in the blackness. From where I walked it was like looking at silent television screens. Ordinary people. But their moving mouths made no sound. The rectangles simply existed in the night as a senseless violence of shapes and colours.

I had moments of panic that she'd never come back.

But of course she did. Her medical practice required it. She said her mother was recovering, and she returned in early August. At Sunningrove the summer term was over and I could do little but think and dream of her, telephone, wait for her calls, plan outings and evenings. The school became a maze of solitary, sunlit corridors for fantasies of her.

Twice we had supper and once an evening walk across the Beacons. She was intensified almost unbearably by the memory of her absence. Something still shook inside me when I thought of it. I had to rediscover her face and body. Sometimes I lost all tenderness. I had to crush the living flesh of her against me, soak up the wetness of her lips. But perhaps it was my own body in whose substance I disbelieved, simply myself I wanted to feel. I don't know. But I'd have these moments of vertigo. They came at me without warning. It was as if I were swimming in a sea and suddenly the sea was not there and I was falling.

And always there would come a time when I seemed to immolate myself in her, a time in which I felt physically fragile, blurring, and from which – for all I knew – I might only wake up dead. I simply drowned in her body (and she so slender!) Her fingers on my back and shoulders seemed to pierce me, as if my frame were bleeding away into hers. I can't explain this. But my loving became like a long, impassioned sleep. Twice I found myself weeping against her breast, I don't know why.

Then some momentary separation – merely a shifting of her

position on the sofa – would start up the hunger, the rage to feel and press and kiss, to extinguish our separateness all over again, until I was crumbled away. There was some fearful frailty in me, I knew. I thought it was physical. I even considered seeing a doctor. But then *she* was a doctor. The next time I saw her, I thought, I'd tell her.

But the next time was different. We'd decided to take a picnic lunch along the Usk one Sunday (the word 'picnic' still nauseates me) following the path from the cottage. The whole day sickens in my memory – the woods' jaded heaviness, the sultry haze in the sky, the lisp of the underfed river, her picnic in its wicker hamper with the red handles. She wore jeans and a T-shirt with 'I love New York' on it (but she'd never been to New York). She went in front of me on the path as if it were too narrow for us to walk abreast, and when I came beside her she kept the picnic basket in her hand between us, isolating herself.

"I'll carry it," I said.

"No."

She wouldn't smile at me, but just stared ahead. Her hair was tied back, so that her cheekbones seemed suddenly very high and hard. She looked absolutely self-contained.

We crossed the river by the old carter's bridge. I reminded her how we'd seen an owl here in early June, but my enthusiasm trickled away against her silence. We spread out the picnic in silence too. It lay on a tablecloth over last year's leaves. I saw she had brought favourites of mine: prawns, raspberries. But when I thanked her she glanced at me with a look of mingled pity and distrust – the look you might give to a wild animal that was dying. It froze me. I didn't look back at her. The picnic lay between us, eerily distinct, untouchable. French bread, butter glinting in silver foil, a thermos, an ivory-handled bread-knife, chicken paté. I could barely pretend to eat it. I talked about anything that came into my head. It wasn't foolish, only irrelevant. It dragged with a lame hopelessness, like something on the run, and finally died. I wondered how we'd ever filled our time with talking. What had we said? Now suddenly there seemed nothing. I joked about Nisbet. She usually enjoyed this. But her mouth barely flickered and my voice grew strained, and at last dwindled. I felt no disgust at my disloyalty to the man. Only this alarm. She answered my talk in monosyllables, simply agreed or disagreed. She was always looking away from me, into the trees, over the river. Everything held her interest except me. Subtly and completely, she had isolated herself. I could no more have touched her than I could have scaled Everest. She ate very little, methodically. All her movements – the cutting of bread, the lifting of a spoon – were oddly formal. I watched the slenderness of her hands slicing the bread. I couldn't raise my eyes farther. Her beauty suddenly frightened me. All the softness of response had drained from her, leaving a face whose bones suddenly looked more powerful than its flesh. I knew she was waiting to speak. I felt the air fanning up in cold, short breaths under my ribs. In the end my voice dwindled away to leave the sound of water ruffling against the piers of the overgrown bridge.

Then the blue gaze turned on me. It was a confusion of preconceived purpose and intruding compassion. She half extended her hand to me, then withdrew it. She said: "Daniel," but the word was without warmth. It was a token of our separateness. It seemed to say: I am Sophia, you are Daniel, we're apart. "Daniel, I have to say something to you which you're going to find hard."

My stare wilted on hers. I couldn't say a word.

She looked away from me. "I just don't think I can take any more."

"How do you mean?"

"I mean this, this . . . I'm not doing you any good, Daniel."

"*Good?*"

"I think you need some other kind of woman. I don't know what kind. But not me. It's been lovely, Daniel. But for me it's just been an ego-trip." She looked up at me but my panic only tightened her voice, drew her farther away. "I don't want it any more, Daniel. I just don't want it."

I couldn't understand what she was telling me. I thought if I didn't understand it, it wouldn't happen. All the invisible threads which bound us had broken, had broken simply by her kneeling there with that look of petrifying resolve. Now I couldn't wrench my gaze from her. Her beauty was terrifying – her cheeks concave under their bones, her mouth a perfect, bow-shaped outlet for unspeakable words.

I said: "Perhaps we should leave it for a while."

"Daniel, I'm going away."

"Away?"

"I'm giving up my practice here. I'm going to London. There's a shortage of . . ."

"London's not far!"

"We can't go on, Daniel. I'm leaving you." Then a spasm of tenderness crossed her face. Her hand reached out towards me, rested sunburnt and impossibly far away on the whiteness of the tablecloth. I stared at it, paralysed. To take it was, for some reason, to accept everything she said, to submit. It lay outstretched between us offering this last atrocious bond. I simply stared at it. I couldn't move. Yet when it withdrew I felt as if the last thread had broken.

"I'll change my job," I said. *I'll just give it up*. My voice had almost disappeared.

"No."

"*I will*."

"Daniel, please understand. You're only making things worse." Her eyes seemed somehow lost to me now. She herself was lost to me. "I can't love you. I want to but I can't."

I stared at her, kneeling in the leaves. The 'I love New York' on her T-shirt looked like an obscure betrayal. "Why can't you?"

"Oh Daniel." She swept a hand against her hair.

"*Tell me*."

"It's just hurtful. I don't know, anyway." She looked away, into the river. "You frighten me."

"*I* frighten *you*?"

"Yes. You make me frightened of myself. But I don't want to talk about it. There's no point. I really don't understand it."

It was still only with my mind that I knew she was going.

The rest of me hadn't heard. I said: "Are you going with Charles?"

"It's nothing to do with Charles. I'm leaving him too."

I followed her stare to the river. The water splashed senselessly on its rocks. "How long will you go for?"

"I'm not coming back, Daniel." She turned on me, irritated now. "Understand. We won't see each other again. *I'm going away for ever.*"

It was the words 'for ever' that stayed. They fluttered desolately. I tried to compass them. Then suddenly they were jerking and tearing inside me. For ever. Were they a wilderness or an abyss? My hands were shaking on my knees. Her absence forever. Always.

"Don't look like that, Daniel. It's not the end of the world."

It is. The end of the world. That is what it is. Never again. Never. Only falling. For ever.

She was crawling in front of me, putting the picnic back into the hamper. We were leaving. Only this replacing of the picnic before. And the short walk down the river. Only these before our parting. Bread, butter, raspberries, thermos. Her hands fumbled as she put them away. She was hurrying, afraid. She was going. And her actual going brought this shock of terror, so that it was at last imaginable: her absence. Breathing the same air somewhere, inhabiting the same planet. But gone. Not there. Even beyond death. *For ever.*

The picnic basket was filled now. She was shaking breadcrumbs out of the tablecloth. I clasped the hamper, holding it against me. If I stayed here she wouldn't go, she couldn't go. She folded up the tablecloth. She didn't look at me. She simply folded the tablecloth over her arm and walked away. But I was terribly cold. A cold vacuum was pressing up inside me, freezing my chest. She was going and it wasn't possible. I was running after her. I don't know if she could hear my voice. *"Please, please."*

I caught her up on the bridge. She turned. For the first time she was standing close to me, breathless. But separate, going away, leaving me to space, to nothing. . . .

71

Yet already, without my knowing precisely when it began, relief was surging through me. I realised – perhaps I had always known – that after all I could keep her, keep her here with me for ever, yes, always. And all the transient warmth of her was suddenly close, there, beautiful near my hands again, this sublime thing. Now my fingers inside the picnic basket were clasping the knife's ivory handle.

Five

In early morning, when the mist steals off the hills and round the hospital, you might imagine the whole institution underwater and its giant trees turned to seaweeds. The windows become portholes onto a void. You can't see from one end of the building to the other. A film of damp covers everything, glistening along the tiled corridors. In the ward kitchens the sugar turns to sodden clods, the vegetables grow fungus overnight and liquid smears of chocolate and Ovaltine spread along the shelves.

Faraday is quiet but vaguely anxious. One of the younger patients has just been released, and was hardly able to contain his joy as he shook the others' hands farewell, and left behind great drifts of envy and unease. Perhaps that's why the roster for washing-up and bedmaking caused acrimony among the elderly inmates, then calmed away into bewilderment. When somebody makes too much noise – when Evans falls over himself or Buddha starts singing – the Boss raps his tarred pipe on the wooden sides of his armchair, and says: "You oughta be in a *mental hospital!*" and Prick and his poker-playing cronies chorus "Nice one, Boss! Nice one!" and the ward relapses into quiet.

Orgill has been out exploring: in the social room, the community hall, the O.T. units of the Chronics. He buys them plastic cups of tea from the cakes counter and sits admiring their old photographs or keepsakes, and telling them how great they're looking. Then he'll burst back into the ward saying "You know, boys, those freaks aren't hardly mad *at all*. There's a guy out there writes poetry with rhythm, scansion, imagery – the whole dicky-bird. And another fellow what was teaching me about prop shafts in coal pits. Whadya say to *that*?" Then he'll settle for a few minutes with Sheldon or Evans or Buddha, or try to concentrate on the television, or start to redecorate the dormitory in a vivid blue emulsion filched from the kitchens. I notice how his hands tremble from the short-term effects of his drugs. They must think him pretty bad. Sometimes I meet him marching down the corridors on the lookout for anything new. His pink and yellow head is always on the verge of a new explosion of delight or surprise. Once I asked him if he'd seen any younger female patients, but he only said: "Young, Prof? Christ no, they're all unfuckably old. But tell you what, there's a student nurse in Social, one of the kids in yellow uniform, you know, and – wow!"

I should have suspected, I suppose, that Sophia wouldn't reappear in that sewing room; and she didn't turn up in any of the public rooms either. She had vanished as completely as if she'd never been here, locked away behind the iron doors of the women's ward. What was she doing? What *was* there to do in there? But whenever I glanced at the television in Faraday I'd think: she's watching this, of course, that's all they do. She's in the same hypnosis as the rest of them, following the shapes and colours over the little screen hour after hour, but seeing her own scenario.

Sordid and pathetic images kept erupting in my mind – the women in the dormitory around her, peeling their stockings and soiled petticoats from withered bodies at night, the immobile Chronics lifted from their urine-stained beds on either side of hers each morning, catheters reinserted, back into the wheelchairs. Foetor of sweat and stale perfume. And in her ears only that lunatic whinnying which lies somewhere between laughter and weeping, and the chattering to the dead. But worst of all was the thought that this was her natural habitat now, the environment fitted to her condition. She probably didn't even notice it.

She was rotting away.

I tried to blink back these images, and make coherent plans. If the atmosphere in Faraday became oppressive, I'd go to the library, which was cramped but usually deserted. The book-shelves form three solid alleyways, all given years ago by a misguided benefactress. There are handsome volumes here, caked in mildew and unread even by the Acutes. Whenever you extract one from its nest of mould, you shake a spume of dust from it before opening the covers gingerly in case they split or the spine cracks like an old bone. But there are banks of illustrated travel books on Germany and southern Italy, and big tomes of nature study, architecture, all kinds of things.

It was here, as I eased out a volume from the middle shelves, that I glimpsed on the far side the stirring of somebody else. The gap left by the book showed only part of a wrist and hand, which vanished immediately, but I felt sure they had been hers. The hand – even in that instant, I noticed – had given up being young, its skin slackened and blemished. I listened for any movement on the far side, but heard nothing. When I squatted down and peered through the serrated apertures left by the books below, I saw nothing either. The absolute silence implied that whoever it was didn't want to be detected. I padded to the end of the stacks and peered round them. When I stopped for a second and listened, I heard the faintest brush of somebody's coat against a shelf. I walked softly down the last, dust-filled alleyway. But there was no more sound. By crouching close to the floor I could see clearly under the raised racks and expected to glimpse her tip-toeing feet. But no. Only on a nearby radiator a book lay open: *Wayside Flowers of the British Isles*. I went to the window and stared down. There was a fire escape – every wall of the hospital is lacerated with them – but nobody on it. Only when I returned to the door did I notice that it was a little ajar, as if somebody had eased it soundlessly open, then slipped away.

But on Sunday morning I saw her again. The patients were discussing who should go to church, Orgill enthusing and Sheldon dithering. Gregory, I noticed, pretended he wasn't in

75

the room at all, withdrew his neck into his hunched shoulders and twisted his head away. The Boss was saying: "You're not getting me to the gospel-shop. As far as I'm concerned, God's just the Head Admin. You see him when you leave, and that's it."

In the rain-soaked garden below, under a black umbrella, she was walking to church. Beneath her knee-length skirt her calves worked the familiar, long-strided gait, but the spring in them was broken, and once or twice her feet trailed in the puddles as if she were overdrugged or desperately tired.

As I reached the garden the rain was falling hard. I saw her three hundred yards away, shaking out her umbrella under the porch of the hospital church – the church which the Victorians built for thirteen hundred bedlamites. I turned up my collar and ran. When I arrived the service had already begun. I found myself in the north transept, staring across a gaunt carcass of a chancel. A few staff nurses were kneeling beside me, but otherwise there was only the booming priest and some twenty Chronics scattered in the pews. Sophia was nowhere in sight. The plain glass in the windows let in a colourless light, which turned everything to common day. One or two wheelchair patients drooped in the aisles. Others had been lifted into pews, and stared vacantly up at the high altar, where a stained-glass Christ hung crucified to redeem the sins they could never have committed. Only Orgill was sitting in the transept opposite, his palms cupped and eyes raised, as if awaiting a divine shower. And Evans behind him, copying. But a part of the nave was obscured from my vision, and I knew she must be kneeling there.

While one of the canticles was ending, I started to edge along my pew towards a better vantage-point. The priest watched me. He was a huge man in a thickly-belted black soutane and his was the only real voice in the church. He bellowed the responses as if he were in lonely conclave with God, and whenever he fell silent all that underpinned his chant was the piping and whining of the twenty Chronics, like babies' souls in limbo. Most of them, I think, confused him with the Almighty.

By the time I'd reached my pew's end and edged into the chancel, he had strode forward and was addressing the church in preparation for Good Friday. The Jews, he said, had done nasty things to Jesus. . . . But beyond him, and beyond the wheelchair patients, there opened out a nave whose desanctified light shone on utter emptiness. Its endless rows of pews tapered back to the west door, through which she might, or might not, have gone. There was nothing else.

The next moment I was wandering down the aisle like any Chronic, oblivious of the psalm swelling on the organ, and staring left and right in case she was doubled up behind a pew. I reached the west porch to find its door unlocked and looked back down the aisle. She must have seen me following her, just as she'd sensed me in the library, and instead of greeting me she'd gone away. I felt my face grown taut, and scarred with lines. I recomposed it. I couldn't tell what I represented to her, whether I revolted or frightened her, or was merely boring. The priest stood blackly before the high altar now, under the redundant Christ, and in the south transept Orgill's hands were lifted high in white supplication, while his thrown-back head shook in a halo of gold.

I let myself through the west door. The rain had stopped and the sky was gashed with an artificial blue. As I lurched out I almost tripped over a figure seated and bent double inside the porch, as if he were praying or being sick. It was Gregory.

"Are you okay?"

He straightened and stared up, trying to focus, fumbling for his glasses. Without them his eyes looked tiny, even sadder, less proportional.

"Oh, it's you. I was just . . . thinking."

"Did a woman come out here?"

"I don't know. I've only been here a few minutes." He stood up shakily, and we walked over the grass between the trees. "What woman?"

"The one I mentioned to you before. You said I should ask Administration." But I didn't want to talk about her any more. I just wanted to go on walking over the grass under the cedars, in the warming sun.

Gregory laced his hands behind his back. He kept glancing at me. "She's hurting you, isn't she?"

It's so rare for a patient to observe and pity anything outside his own pain that this moved me. I touched his arm. "It'll be all right." I couldn't explain about her. I changed the subject back to him. He looked as wretched as I felt. "You were in a bad way when I came into the porch, weren't you? But there's nothing in that church, you know. Just pews and stone and old books. It's nothing to worry about."

"I was sheltering from the rain."

"I thought maybe you were ill – or even praying."

"I?" His hands unlaced again. "I can't pray. That was just dizziness." We walked on for a minute or two. Suddenly he said: "Do you know what I heard when I was sitting there? You've got some big-voiced man in there, haven't you? I heard *Be ye sure that the Lord he is God: it is he that hath made us, and not we ourselves.*" His hands flickered together unbearably. "I thought: then whose fault is it? We're just *things*. You can't be guilty if you're just a thing . . . Things don't burn in Hell. My father used. . . . Perhaps I was praying, then. But nothing ever comes. You see, even a thing must have some sort of body, mustn't it?" His voice dwindled. "I get confused."

"But Gregory, you're guilty of less than anyone I know. And you've got just as much body as I have." Yet I understood what he meant: the sensation of being on the edge of nothingness, wanting to move away, or not wanting, or not knowing which.

"Then why should I always be feeling this. . . . Why should I?"

"This what?"

"This thing of not being there. Or if I am, I don't deserve to be, so it's better not to be. People see inside me, you know, right inside."

"They don't."

"Yes they do. Not you maybe, Daniel, maybe you don't." We stopped under the outer wall. He was shaking in the sun. "But the Boss, for instance, he looks right inside me. When he

78

looks at me I can feel it physically. I seem to have no forehead and he's looking in."

We started to walk back. I put my arm round him. He felt spindly as a clothes rack. I said: "The Boss doesn't see anything."

"Not if you avoid his eyes, then he doesn't. But if you let him stare at you, he'll gimlet in. You see, he knows . . . he knows I'm thin. He knows he can get in. You're not as thin as me. Oh God, am I making sense?"

On the night of the pop concert Gregory had some sort of breakdown. He never spoke of it afterwards, even to me. He probably couldn't have explained it if he'd wanted. Before curtain-up in the community hall I sat in his empty chair, hoping they hadn't put him on electro-convulsive. Because that terrifies him: he's afraid they'll reduce him to a film of ashes, to the nothing that he says he really is.

The hall was filled with Chronics and staff, and with the hospital's League of Friends, who mingled with the patients as parents might mix with their children. I scanned the doors in the hope of glimpsing Sophia, but it was impossible to watch all the entrances at once. Most of the four hundred patients were already crammed into the room, and the lights were dimmed. I was seated in a caucus of Acutes, who had insulated themselves from the Chronics this evening, fearful of contagion.

The curtain parted on a makeshift stage. Four singers in harlequin coats and yellow masks stood in front of the microphones. A brilliant concentration of light from behind us lent them ghoulish height and intensified the iridescence of their clothes. Then the hall was swallowed up in their clashing and roaring – the amplification system had been turned too high. For a while the audience was drubbed into silence and immobility, except for ingrained mumblings and tics. But even in this cacophany a few of the Chronics fell into drugged sleep, their chairs twisted askew. Others became bored or withdrawn, complained to the air. They punctuated the music with shouts and indecipherable greetings. But most were transfixed in their chairs, mesmerised by the patterns of the rainbow-coloured people trapped and gyrating in the light, and simply watched the changing shape of things, as if a television had jerked into more drastic perspective.

But the response that emanated from this audience was only a spasmodic Babel, and into this the singers despairingly poured their souls. The audience began fraying at the edges. Some of the patients picked up their plastic chairs and replaced them elsewhere, others tried to sit in the laps of the sane. Orgill and Buddha joined the Chronics ambling round the walls. Buddha started waltzing with himself, lifting his hand from time to time in a graceful gesture of peace and dangling one of Orgill's half-finished cigarettes. The show continued for its own sake. The singers told their stock jokes, couldn't adapt them to the mad. The staff laughed pityingly. The music pulsed and crashed out again, the harlequins bawled and rocked.

Sheldon suddenly stood up. "I can't take this any more." He squirmed between the chairs. "The noise is getting inside my head. I'm going back to the ward." The Boss was beating time with his pipe on the chair in front of him. His head swayed watchfully to the rhythm, crossed by a little smile.

Orgill took Sheldon's seat. He jerked a thumb at the stage, shouting against the noise. "These guys are into some real crappy stuff."

"Yeah," said Evans. "Crap."

The music stopped. The lead singer grabbed the micro-phone, trying for the participation of his phantasmal audience. "Good evening, one-and-all. Hi-there-everybody! Now let's see some talent from the floor. Who's gonna give us a song? Show us all watcha can do. Get famous. There you go, sir, come right up."

A colossal, bloated man I didn't know was clambering on to the stage. The singer pushed the microphone at him. "You're on your own now, sir. Give 'im the backing, boys." The drummer rolled out a crescendo. The microphone had disap-peared into the man's spade-like fist, which he brought hal-tingly up to his face. He stood foursquare to the audience, like a monstrous baby, and gazed above our heads, while a claque of friends broke into yells below him. Then he sang unaccompanied in a gravelly, tuneless voice:

> *Daisy, Daisy, give me your answer do,*
> *I'm half crazy, all for the love of you,*
> *They wrap you up in paper bags*
> *And tie you up with string*
> *They do, they wrap you up in paper bags*
> *And tie you up and tie you up*
> *They tie you up, they tie you up,*
> *They tie you up, tie you up. . . .*

He was ushered to the side of the dais and descended in lumbering jerks. The sane could not look at him. The Chronics broke into cheers and desultory clapping. While he was returning, I found an empty chair far to one side, from where I could see the audience. Most of the seats were still filled, and as the stage jokes proliferated again the intermingled faces of the staff and the patients became a grotesque counterpoint of wholeness and decay. That's how it's always been here, of course, I've been amongst it for years. But because of Sophia the contrast between the Chronics and the Acutes, the lunatic and the precariously sane, struck me now with despair. The faces of the sane, lifted towards the stage, were variegated, lit, seemed momentarily rare and miraculous. But those of the mad were merely masks for people eroded behind them. Whatever expressions they wore had petrified there long ago in the vacancy or agony that had last consumed them.

I couldn't see her. Nearby was a dense bloc of women patients. Many were in wheelchairs or clutched babywalkers. They were rocking and gesticulating to the music, beating time with their handbags or unlit cigarettes. A few of their faces had uncrumpled into lewd grins; their hands waved and blew kisses at the singers.

The music stopped again. The leader rattled into the microphone: "Okay, one-and-all, give the lads a rest, shall we, and let's have talent from the floor. Who's gonna be the next Elvis, then? Let's be hearing from you. . . ."

But nobody came up. The big man got to his feet again, but was pulled back by his friends.

"C'mon, folks. Let's have a song now. Twang a few heart-strings, ladies, or one of you fellows start the feet tapping. Who's it gonna be? Let's be hearing . . ."

There was a trickle of clapping as somebody came up from the darkness of the hall's centre. She took the microphone on the far edge of the dais, hesitated a moment, then stepped into its light. Isolated in that white pool, thin as a waif, she faltered to the front of the stage, while all the changed lines of her face were deepened by the glare's cruelty, and her hair shifted around her in a dead brown dust. She looked like an ancient child. She turned to the band, as if expecting them to accompany a song they couldn't anticipate, then realised she was alone. Her body, in its drab green dress, seemed already drained. Sophia balanced the microphone awkwardly at her fingertips, frowned at it; smoothed her dress round her hips with the other hand.

Then she pushed out her song into the quiet. It came in a low, parched filament of voice:

> *It's easy to see*
> *Why all who learn to know you love you*
> *You're gentle and kind*

The brilliance of the light, and the audience, and her isolation there, intensified her. She stopped frowning into the microphone as she sang, and settled an unfocused gaze on the back of the hall. Although she stood in the same circle of light as had the gangling pop singers, she might have belonged to a different species. She was pathetically thin and coarsened, and it could only have been a trick of my memory, or of the stage vista, that in some corrupted way, with those wasted cheekbones and enormous, blue-ice eyes fixed on thin air, she seemed to be – yes – still beautiful.

> *I'm always dreaming of you*
> *No matter what I do I can't forget you*
> *Sometimes I wish that I had never met you*

82

Her eyes swivelled slowly in my direction, but stared over my head, and God knows what she was seeing. The next moment she'd stepped out of the white pool and back into the dark.

Ten minutes later the concert was over and the doors jammed with patients and nurses. I tried to press and wriggle through the tangle of unco-ordinated Chronics and wheelchairs congesting the door nearest to Sophia, then made instead for the clearest exit and ran round the corridors to the women's ward. By the time I reached it the patients were already trickling through the iron doors, supervised by a hefty orderly. I waited. The faces passing me were all old, even older than their years. Inside I could see their white heads moving down the middle of a long, bare dormitory, whose sheeted beds looked like marble slabs.

Then her voice behind me said as if to herself: "You here?"

She looked smaller but warmer than she had on stage, more actual. She didn't try to pass me, but bent down to shake something out of her shoe. For some reason I thought: I still love you. But I only said: "You were going to meet me."

She straightened and faintly smiled. "Why?" The question came impenetrable, without emotion of any sort. Just a word.

I had to think why. I was confused by her face. "You said you'd write a story. You were going to remember."

"Story." She seemed to be thinking. She stooped and took off her shoe again, peered into it. "Is there a splinter?"

I looked. "No, I don't see one. Sophia, do you . . . ?"

"No splinter? None at all?" She replaced the shoe. "Wait."

Then she went through the door, walking fast, and the starched bulk of the orderly came between us. I saw her brown head passing quickly down the aisle of beds, away. I leant back against the corridor wall. Its tiles were clammy against the palms of my hands. I knew she wouldn't return, but waited there simply because she'd asked me to. The last patients shuffled through the door and the orderly heaved it shut. The reverberation echoed on and on down the corridor. I continued standing there, supported by the wall. I wondered how many minutes or hours would elapse before I allowed myself to leave. A numbness was spreading through me. I started to shiver. After ten minutes the curtain in the door panel shot aside and the orderly's face appeared. The door grated open and I turned my back with affected indifference, expecting to be questioned. But instead there came an odd, furtive tapping at my elbow.

"Here it is." Sophia was handing me a sliver of papers. She looked childishly proud.

I stared at them in my hands, not knowing what they were. The door clanged like a vault as she went back in.

I remained there, leaning against the wall. The papers shook in my hands. I glanced at them. I became utterly confused. They were not handwritten, but neatly typed. Slowly, then in a nervous flood, I began to hope. All her mental force seemed to have passed into the written word instead of into speech. The sentences read exactly as if they'd been composed ten years ago – her authentic voice. Momentarily I imagined she might be suffering from one of those schizophrenias which fall cleanly, suddenly, leaving the memory unimpaired like a cool lake of the past just beneath the deranged present. Then I examined the foolscap paper. It was yellow with age; and when I ran my fingers over the type it left no fresh smear of ink. Perhaps the thing had been composed years ago, as a cathartic exercise for some analyst or other. It was impossible to tell, completely mystifying.

This is what she had written:

Six

I came to Cruwenath on the invitation of Dr Robertson, who passed out of medical school the year before I did. I'd like to think I was a bright instance of sexual equality in the professions, but I wasn't. Many of Robertson's patients were gynae and obstetric cases, the usual fodder for women doctors. I was female first and medical second. I should have called myself Dr Vagina Brown.

It was the Welsh hills in summer which decided me to stay. Just here they resemble long, man-made earthworks, and rise to about 2000 feet. They are mostly pastureland: Friesians and every kind of sheep. The streams are very clear, and wear away the soil to a flat rock surface which looks like paving-slabs. There is far less undergrowth than in the West Country, and the trees in this solitude are magnificent.

I never got over an excitement about answering night calls from these hills. The farmhouses are lonely and sometimes could only be reached by mud tracks between the fields. The people accepted me with the misplaced faith of patients for any doctor, and my role on these occasions – somewhere between Paul Revere and Florence Nightingale – tickled my more idiotic fancy, so that the most gauche remarks about my womanly stamina only made me flush and smile.

What I hadn't bargained for was the social isolation. I became deeply conscious of how English I was, and how bourgeois. But being the victim of my country's class contrasts only made me hate them the more. And I did make friends. I was put on exhibition at local supper parties as 'our lady doctor', and I grew fond of several farming families.

But I think all this drew me closer to Charles. His parents had been friends of my father years before, and at first he asked me out in a spirit of dutifulness. Charles had a languid charm, and was considerate in a distant sort of way. I felt secure with him. Even when he slept with me it seemed an act of courtesy rather than of passion, and this appealed to some part of my nature. But he had no idea that the genital sensitivity of women might be different from that of men. He once told me that sexual foreplay wasn't his scene, as if it was snooker or perhaps a perversion.

But it's frightening to write like this about somebody you've held in your arms. I never loved Charles, but I was often happy with him. We used to go to London together – it was like bursting into a world more nearly my own – and twice we took summer holidays on the Algarve. Charles was quite uninterested in foreign countries and peoples, but he never derided them. Cruelty and sarcasm were outside his nature, and even his air of superiority was in some way a sham: not self-protective, simply an unconscious inheritance.

What he saw in me I still don't know. He used to say we 'spoke the same language', which faintly alarmed me; and with his London friends he enjoyed the liberal image of my being a doctor. But beyond that, I'm not sure. He was probably bored. As for me, I felt obscurely flattered. I've never had much success with men. My figure's too scraggy and my hair almost mouse-coloured. Until I was about fourteen people thought I was a boy. I suspect my personality lacks sex. I'm too matter-of-fact or something. In medical school the trainee doctors were always confiding their affairs to me, as if I didn't count. My one good feature is my eyes, which are large and greyish blue, but they're set in such an irregular face that they only have surprise value. I just thank God (if only I believed in Him) that I'm emotionally independent. The idea of marriage frightens me; and after delivering a few dozen other people's babies, the appeal of motherhood has got drowned in their screams and blood.

I'd been two years in my practice when this strangeness happened. It only came the more violently for intruding into a life of matured routine. I don't pretend this life was unpleasant, but I'd subconsciously come to feel that I invited only ordinary things to happen to me. I had always been what my mother called 'a sensible girl'. I inhabited the expected.

Then this fervid-looking man was hovering near my clinic door. His arms had a nervous way of jerking back stiffly from his body and his face was dead white. Within two minutes I found I'd agreed to have lunch with him. He looked so pitifully embarrassed that I thought he must be seeking help: I imagined V.D., although he didn't look the type.

Then little by little, sitting in a crowded restaurant, I realised that he had nothing particular to divulge. He seemed simply to want to talk. I was absolutely mystified. He apologised for everything: for the noise, the food, his appearance, for inviting me at all. He even apologised about the weather. He was so jittery that I momentarily thought him retarded. He poured out questions on every period and aspect of my life and absorbed the answers with a peculiar intentness. And he seemed to have at his fingertips all the silliest layman's myths about my profession. What a wonderful, selfless calling it must be, he said – he even mentioned 'love for your patients' – and how inspiring to be doing so much good in the world. I was beginning to find him distasteful. His forelock of dark hair agitated over his brows and his knife kept mulching cannelloni which he never ate. I told him roundly that half the patients at my clinic were just lonely or neurotic, and how as a houseman in hospital I'd often felt it would be kinder to machine-gun half the geriatric wards rather than continue feeding the life in those rotted bodies.

When I asked him about his own job he stuttered and prevaricated. He was the English and games master at a local prep school, but he seemed to find this profoundly demeaning. He'd already been there eleven years, but he said he was leaving at any moment and sent out a flurry of bravado about new posts. The whole subject plunged him into an inexplicable turmoil, and I could tell that half the time he was lying. Then he started talking about the homesickness of the smaller boys, and did so with such intense sadness that I wondered about his own childhood. But when I asked if he'd suffered like that himself he only joked: "Are you doing a psychiatric job on me?"

And I suppose I was. He seemed to relax a little then, as much as he ever did. Suddenly his talk was a flood of loves and enthusiasms. Music, Italy, French architecture, Russian literature. He poured them out in a kind of jubilant fusillade. It was peculiarly infectious. Personally I find Mahler morbid and Dostoevsky impossible, but this strange man's pleasure in them was powerful and rather moving. The whole conversation became unnervingly vivid. I couldn't imagine anybody else talking like this – certainly not Charles. But Daniel made you feel the world was actually different from the one you experienced. It was more vital and precious. If you didn't agree with him you felt cloddish. If you did, it was oddly enhancing. There was a time in our conversation when I realised I no longer found him pathetic but rather awesome. It was an extraordinary leap in feeling, and I hoped I didn't show it.

I suppose it was because I'd never seen him in other company that at first I assumed he must behave like this with everybody. But I realised that he hadn't so much as glanced at his food, let alone eaten any. His eyes simply never left my face. They were dark brown, under heavy brows. They stared with a kind of burning softness. Then the truth dawned on me. It was amazing, I thought, after all these years. I even started to blush. Nobody had ever looked at me like that before. I was a little shaken. He was good-looking in a dark slightly disconcerting way. He had a long, bony face and nose and full lips. And his eyes had this restless intensity.

My thoughts came blundering out. I said: "You haven't eaten a *thing*. Don't you usually? Doesn't your girlfriend feed you?" But for some reason I knew he was alone.

He looked confused and his gaze dropped from my face. He

muttered how his affairs always fell to pieces, then said: "What about your boyfriend?"

I watched his expression as I answered, and saw it momentarily convulsed by the most extraordinary pain. His eyelids winced shut and his lips prised back from his teeth. It was perfectly astonishing. I thought: I've only known him for half an hour, and he's in love with me. But the next moment he'd recomposed himself.

"What does he do?"

"He's a house agent."

"Oh."

It did seem drab, and his tone of voice made it a crime. What had he expected me to say? 'My boyfriend is a duke, the Poet Laureate, a multi-millionaire'? But it was impossible to know what he expected. His stare was travelling over my body now, and made me uncomfortable. I might just as well not have dressed.

In any case, it was time for me to leave. I knew he'd ask to see me again, but I didn't know what I'd answer. When I accepted, I thought it was for his sake. Perhaps it was. I can't remember now.

I think I have a puritan desire to be useful. For all my dislike of shibboleths like 'caring' and 'dedicated', it's the fulfilling of obvious needs which keeps my work happy. But there come times when a certain hopelessness descends, and the next few days were like this. In the Welsh ex-mining valleys the average working-class wife falls victim to a fierce stress. Even market-towns like Cruwenath, apparently so relaxed and ordinary, sometimes seem a welter of incurable pain. These mornings my clinic was filled with those sad women who believe their stomach or vaginal symptoms are purely physical, although the lightest touching on their personal lives exposes a hopeless vortex of tensions. They sat beyond my desk with their mouths twitching and hands wrenching together, looking at me as if I were Christ. So of course I felt a fraud. Probably a lifetime's psychoanalysis wouldn't help them. You just give them a placebo or prescribe an antibiotic like some canting wizard with no spells left, and you know they'll be back in a few weeks. Others transfer their tensions to their children and endow them with imaginary ailments. "Doctor, baby keeps making this little wheezing . . ."

For some reason my temper and sensitivity were exacerbated these few days. It was like being a student again. I got upset by the futility of things. A visit to one of the patients in hospital – a Cruwenath shopkeeper called Jarrett who was dying of pancreatic cancer – was unbearably depressing. As a student I had imagined that dying must be different in quality from living: that death was elevating. But of course, it isn't. Jarrett was the kind of man people call 'chirpy'. He lay propped up in bed entering figures into his account books. He had less than a month to live. At first I thought this fastidiousness signified concern for the family he would leave behind (a gross wife and two teenage daughters). Then it dawned on me that this wasn't so. No, he simply couldn't conceive of death at all, couldn't grasp that 'T. R. Jarrett, Tobacconist and Confectioner' might one day not exist. He never even asked me for a prognosis on his disease. He merely went on doing what he had always done: filling in figures. I found his wife sitting by his bedside that evening, and overheard what must have been one of their last conversations together: "What were the takings on filter-tip last week then?. . . Forty-seven, sixty, shouldn't be bad . . . an outside rack for the local weeklies. . . ."

It wasn't death that depressed me: just that nothing alive seemed to be dying. The evening Daniel came I felt utterly worn-out. I had a bath and drank three cups of coffee, trying to wake myself up. I had no idea what to wear. I didn't know if he planned to drive me to a five-star Gloucester hotel or to the nearest Chinese take-away.

Then, when he arrived, I felt again that exotic sensation of being worshipped and wondered at. Charles never much noticed what I wore, or even how I looked. But now everything I did or said was the focus of almost agonised attention. The speed with which I got used to this was a bit disgusting. I suddenly understood the self-confidence of attractive women.

We drove to Monmouth through the night hills. His car was a coupé, the car of the solitary. I suspect it had been cleaned and polished for my benefit because the seams of the dashboard were brown with betraying dust. In Monmouth we parked outside one of those restaurants which could be a haunt only for the tasteless rich. But he'd booked a table here, and a minute later we were in the lobby, ogling a framed menu that was brutally expensive.

Daniel was always feeling things at times when I was impervious, but there now came a moment of pure synchronism. The instant his hands touched my shoulders I knew it wasn't a casual gesture, and the next second I felt this impassioned writhing, pleading of his fingers down my arms. His hands were trembling through the silk. It was a kind of sensual prayer. I could hear his breathing faint and light behind me, and my own breath quickened too. I was a little surprised. In a minute his fingers came burning between mine and my arms had started to tingle. I found myself hovering. I wanted to tell him something, but couldn't find the words. So I leant back gently against his chest, my face near his neck. I could feel his erection flat against my buttocks. I wouldn't have dared take him in my arms at this time, but it was easy to slip into this coward's embrace. Which was, I suppose, what I meant to tell him: 'I like you, but I'm afraid.'

The acknowledgement must have relaxed us. Soon I felt our table was the only living one in that pretentious restaurant. Daniel wore a carefully-pressed black suit which he probably reserved for school chapel and me. But he managed to look indefinably eccentric, with his harrowing eyes and that shaking mass of black hair. He spoke in breathy bursts and there was a softening tinge of the North Country in his voice. Yet he didn't look quite English. His eyes and nose (and name) were Jewish, but I never asked him about this. Perhaps that is why he seemed in sharper focus than the people sitting around us. In fact that was his disturbing quality. He was quite unlike other men I'd known. He never mentioned politics or the weather or sport. I doubt if he noticed them. Instead he'd ask what I felt about religion or love or Beethoven's Violin

91

Concerto. It was desperately demanding. I'd discover thoughts and feelings which I didn't know I'd ever had. He stirred up an ocean of the half-forgotten or suppressed. You'd find yourself telling him things that you hadn't even told yourself; sometimes they seemed to be his sort of things rather than yours. It was confusing.

But his sensitivity to me was mimosa-like. The moment I looked bemused by his abstractions he'd deprecate himself and joke (an odd thing: he joked but never laughed) or ask me instead what I felt about toadstools or the Welsh castles. Then he'd join in (if I'd felt anything about them) with that fierce poetic intensity of his, or suddenly be reminded of something else and digress into the north Italian gardens or the Black Forest or the Greek temples of Sicily. He wasn't intellectual so much as violently emotional and imaginative, with an almost photographic memory. Sometimes I felt uncannily as if I was leafing through high-coloured illustrations. Then suddenly he'd ask out of the blue: "Why on earth have you never been married?" – and I'd feel a spurious dignity in his disbelief that no-one had ever asked me.

I don't know who was hypnotising who. His stare only left my face to travel over my neck and breasts (such as they are) and then return to my eyes. It's perturbing how you come to take your identity from somebody else's gaze. I have quite a solid sense of myself, I think. If I hadn't, I'd have turned into a kind of worshipped bauble. Because I didn't have to do or say anything with him. It was enough simply that I was there. He enacted this dance of talk and love around me, while I remained like a totem at its centre. Maybe I was decadent to bask in it. Yet sometimes, strangely, I felt that I became a little what he believed me to be. I softened. Perhaps I even took on some kind of beauty because of him. But no – more likely I just took on foolishness. I certainly contracted several silly mannerisms. I caught myself simpering and putting my head to one side in an idiotic pastiche of some film star. I was trying to enter the country of his vision.

A little later I heard myself giving the impression that I'd been away on numerous holidays with men. It was then, with a seriousness too plain to dismiss, that Daniel joked about wanting to go away with me himself. We were left staring at one another in silence. I couldn't collect myself for a decision. And he looked as if he was on a knife-edge. "*Please.*"

It was a tormented whisper. The force of need in it was frightening. It prevented its own fulfilment. I said: "Have you never gone away with anyone?" – and the moment passed.

He talked about expeditions with a schoolmaster and with his father, but his voice had lost all its shine and he looked stricken, as if this golden land of our holiday was dimming and receding from him visibly. I've never fallen in love, and of all the things most difficult for people like me to understand is that our own mediocrity can actually attract anything so absolute. It was alternately fatuous and awesome.

I laid a hand on his. "Do you want to come for a walk on Saturday?" Why I asked him at the same time as Charles, I don't know. It wasn't just instantaneous pity. In spite of his obsession, Daniel was in some way too formidable to pity. I think I wanted to resolve something about them both, as if I was collating different parts of my nature. "Are you free?"

He was busy adoring my outstretched hand (which was leathery from spring gardening). "Yes, I'm free."

I said: "Are your parents country people too?"

Then I mentioned his mother: and the effect of this was very strange. For the first and only time that he was with me his eyes grew vague and glazed, and his voice, as he answered my softening questions, grew softer and softer too, as if he was physically retreating into a long distance. "Is she dead? . . . Yes, she is. . . . A long time ago? . . . Yes. . . ."

Quite mystifying. I could have felt the upset without my sketchy training in psychology. We never mentioned her again. But I can tell she belongs to the living dead: she continues in his mind.

You notice the clouds in this country. I suppose that's because of the hills' bareness. More than half your field of vision seems to be sky. In winter you feel there's nothing between you and the Atlantic, and the winds drive the scud at double-speed, like a giant cyclorama. This makes the stillness of some spring days solemn by contrast, and that afternoon was one of these – balmy and warm, with lambs bleating operatically in the fields.

By now I was feeling a fool for asking Charles and Daniel together. It wasn't hard to imagine their reactions. Charles: 'Where on earth did you meet that emaciated chap with the Northern lingo?' Daniel: 'You *can't*, Sophia. He's *cardboard*. How *can* you? Oh Sophia . . .' But it was too late to cancel.

Charles and Angela arrived for a makeshift lunch. Long before I knew Angela my father's relatives used to prefix her with 'dear old', as if she was already marked for a hearty spinsterhood. But dear old Angela's brusque manner concealed shrewdness and strong attachments, including a protective devotion to Charles. I was never sure what she felt about me.

Today, for some reason, I wondered if Charles envisaged any future with me. He rarely expressed his feelings, and we had an unspoken pact not to use the word 'love'. I assumed he wanted to keep us as we were. I hoped so. But now, when Angela and I were alone in the kitchen, I found myself asking her: "How's the estate agency going? Charles looks a bit tired."

"He's tired when it's busy."

"Does he ever think of changing? He never talks of it."

"Charles doesn't like change. He prefers developing things from inside."

I went on slicing tomatoes.

She said: "Who's this man coming this afternoon?"

I wondered what train of thought had led her to this. "Oh he's a master at the local prep school. Bit of a dump apparently. Came to the clinic with a torn ligament. Quite clever, I think, a bit shy."

"Who's shy?" It was Charles' voice from the room next door.

Angela shouted: "This fellow – whatsisname? – Pashley, coming this afternoon."

Charles peered in. "Sophia, who is he?"

Angela went on shouting, as if Charles was still in the other room. "He's one of Sophia's patients. No need to be jealous. The Hippocratic oath forbids what you're thinking."

I thought jealousy outside Charles's nature, but Angela knew better. Her bantering tone was just faintly tinged with conciliation. I suppressed a joke about Daniel not being on my patients' register, and began to feel uncomfortable.

This discomfort grew as the afternoon wore on. Daniel had envisaged being alone with me, and looked utterly crestfallen. Even Charles seemed restless, and suddenly put his arm round me as we were walking. This was quite unlike him. Charles deplored affectionate display in public places, and to him a tributary of the Usk was public. It was a gesture of ownership, of course, not of love; but it only increased my unease. As Daniel walked in front of us I could tell by the set of his shoulders and neck that he realised who Charles was. It's extraordinary how expressive backs can be. Daniel's seemed to rear up and envelop half his head. He might have been walking through sleet.

But the river was beautiful. The beeches and ashes were all out, and filled with sun. The water came high over its rocks. Walking with Charles in such places always seemed a bit pointless. We might as well have been in Cruwenath high street. He talked interminably about housing. He didn't want to leave Daniel out, and so marched alongside him in a kind, misguided way. He was terribly boring. All through the fern glen and past the small cascades we heard about the new three-bedroom units on bus-routes, the advantages of auction over private purchase and the impact of low-cost endowment mortgage schemes.

Suddenly Daniel said: "Look! A tawny owl."

And there it was, housed in an oak tree (without a mortgage) high and alone in the water-clashing glen. It was the kind of sight that Daniel loves. The owl released him. He talked to it in its own language, mimicking its sharp, two-note cry then hooting through interlaced hands. When it didn't respond he surprised it by imitating the sadder hoot of the long-eared owl (the other species can't hoot apparently) and scrabbled under the oak to find its disgorged pellets, flecked with beetle-wings and the tiny bones of consumed voles. As we went on, he wandered between the path and the stream, fascinated by things which the rest of us would never have noticed. He seemed to extend the river's life. He was riveted by the tints and formations of the water over the rocks, and slithered down a bank to locate wild balsam and a poisonous clutch of sulphur tuft mushrooms. He jokingly offered one of these to Charles, who wasn't amused, then described kingfishers which he'd seen picking sticklebacks out of the Derwent and bolting them head-first (so the fins didn't stick.) Charles and Angela trudged on looking bored. Occasionally one of them said "How interesting" or "Really?" in a tone of mutual soullessness. I've never seen them in a worse light and I realised that – yes – Charles was a little jealous.

Only once Angela said: "You must have been brought up in the country."

But Daniel's "Yes" was fraught with the inhibition he always showed when talking about his childhood, even with me.

The rabbit that lay in the river was virtually dead. One hind leg was broken under it, and its body already stiffening with cold. But as we crowded round, it became the focus for a disgusting charade. I didn't realise how much Charles had been affected by Daniel until he knelt beside the creature and talked about its pain and beauty. He obviously thought that sensitivity was the order of the day. I nearly retched. He shoots rabbits every other weekend. Whereas Daniel, for some reason, had to lounge overhead with his hands in his pockets and be rational about vermin and the plight of farmers. Each might have been parodying the other. I felt furious and humiliated, because I knew this farce was being enacted for me. Meanwhile the rabbit was dying.

I leant over it, avoiding their faces. "It's kinder to kill it." I checked its broken leg, and it winced back at me. It had beautiful, white-flecked eyes. For the moment it was the only decent creature on the scene. I kept my stare down, waiting for one of the men to take it away. My eyes started to smart. I thought: how ridiculous, last week a patient died in my arms and I didn't shed a tear, and now I'm going to cry over this damn rabbit. I got up and walked off. Daniel and Angela followed. Everybody knew it was Charles who'd kill it. I doubted if Daniel could kill a woodlouse, and his wordly stance wouldn't have fooled anybody.

But Charles had pretended to feelings he never had.

I walked back far ahead of them, with Angela. She was rather silent. Her only comment on Daniel was "I should think a little goes a long way."

It was soon after this that I applied for a partnership in the East End of London, and was accepted. I wanted to breathe another air (even if it was polluted) and my social concern was bolstered by the thought of doctoring Indians beaten up by the National Front in Spitalfields. For a few days I procrastinated; but looking back, I think Daniel affected my eventual decision to leave. Perhaps I even had a slight, premonitory fear, if you believe that sort of thing.

But in any case, I wouldn't have escaped him, he was so obsessed. His declaration would simply have taken place in Greenwich or Hackney instead of in my garden at Cruwenath. As it was, I remember this moment standing beside the choked-up goldfish pond in the evening, while he was crouched at my feet staring at the water. Then I felt the tips of his fingers brushing mine. I knew something had happened in him. He stood up like a ghost rising. I've never seen such appalled loss on any face. The tension of his jaw muscles had pulled his mouth slightly open, and sent all his gaunt cheeks' lines zig-zagging down under bulging voids of eyes. It was frightening and piteous.

"What's this?" He lifted up my hand with my mother's family ring on it.

"Oh Daniel! I just wear this for my patients . . ."

Then I laughed to cover my fear, and went on laughing and teasing him until those ghastly lines reassembled into under-standing; and suddenly he was kissing me in a shock-wave of relief which turned to craving. If I tried to separate myself for an instant he would gather me back against him. His kisses fell on my cheeks and neck and hair with a reverence whose absurdity was already dimming to me. Oh God.

That was the most extraordinary thing in the following weeks: how his vision of me contained us. At first it seemed comical that whole evenings passed in which his kisses simply toured my face on a kind of holy pilgrimage. Once, for two or three hours, he did nothing but caress my shoulders, as if they were amputated from the rest of my body; when his fingers brushed my breasts a look of pained longing crossed his face, but a whole week passed before he took them in his hands. We might have been high school kids on our first, tentative exploration. But after a while – and this was the strange thing – I began to feel as he did. I became embarrassed, almost innocent. I started to rediscover my own body in his worship and inhibition. It trembled at his detection of my calves, breasts. Where other men would have crushed or ignored, he lingered in astonished tenderness. Little by little, I suppose, I lost my self-knowledge. I began to see with his eyes. We were closeted together, there was no-one else to witness. I started to feel proud and even – yes – beautiful.

But the next morning I'd stare in the mirror in order to pull myself together (as my mother would say) and I'd see the familiar shambles. I'm emphatically not beautiful. My face is too bony, and highly irregular. I suppose I'm a bit on the masculine side. My hair's virtually lustreless, whatever conditioner I use. I even have poor teeth.

I dare say the contrast made it all worse, and that if I'd been handsome I'd have accepted his tribute as a permanent truth. But as it was, I colluded like a traitor in his fantasy. It didn't affect my daytime work yet. My beauty, as it were, came and went. And it all happened over an amazingly short stretch of time: a few evenings, a weekend or two. One Sunday we went to the sea somewhere beyond Cardiff. It was a blustery day, completely clouded over, but I honestly believe my presence made him think it sunlit. We spent an hour huddled together under our towels like two anorexics. Whenever we embraced I imagined you could hear the bones clacking. Another weekend we went to the theatre in Bristol, and I think he spent the whole time, literally, watching me in the darkness out of the corner of his eye. I was wearing a dowdy, off-the-shoulder dress, and it was enough for him if he could gaze simply at an isolated part of me – a hand, an arm – which had fallen into his vision. When we discussed the play afterwards, he hadn't heard a word.

This intensity never slackened. He behaved as if each evening was our last on earth. Often I could accept his love as something outside myself. But at other times, when his kissing went very deep, or when his fingers overran my whole body and came trickling high up my thighs, I'd suddenly feel wrenched out of true, sucked into the vortex of those eyes and that voice. I've never been so confused. I thought I was on the verge of what's called falling in love. I suddenly had a different sense of what I was. It was as if the bottom had dropped out of my daylight nature, the nature I had accepted as mine, and that instead this – this writhing, crying, ecstatic thing – was actually me. It was more vivid and real, and more alarming, than anything I'd ever experienced.

Yet I refused him entry. I think I was terrified of being owned. I felt myself, my wholeness, to be there still inside me. So long as I refused him, he couldn't absolutely invade or possess me. If he'd insisted, I'd have succumbed. But he was a mixture of terrible passion and unearthly respect. Perhaps that's what in the end was unendurable: being sacred.

And there was his own fear too. Sometimes, after deep kissing, he'd disengage his lips with a panicky, lost look. You might have thought my mouth the entrance to Hell. Once he said he was frightened of his own extinction. I couldn't always tell if he was happy or afraid. Yet at other times he buried himself against my stomach or breasts, and sucked there like a baby. He'd stopped knowing or caring what to do with his life.

I found it easy to go on seeing Charles. Charles was my hold on sanity, on ordinary things. He was kindly and distant. He went in and out of me like a commuter with a season ticket. He couldn't have owned a breath of me. In every way these two men touched me in different parts. One was conditioning, the other life. At least at the time I thought so. One was simply my mask; the other my reality, the release of my inner alarmingness, of my guts or sex or heart. Or whatever it was.

In early July Mama had her operation – a stay of execution – and I spent three weeks with her in the flat at Poole. We passed the time sitting on her verandah in the sun, reading or talking, and sometimes walked gingerly along the sea front, she with her hand on my arm, complaining "Who'd have thought it would come to this?"

Mama and I were never that close. I was what she called a model child – a dangerous thing to be. I resented her for having dominated me (as I thought), but this resentment came long after I'd left home and I think she never sensed it. Now, in her frailty, it was easier to love her. Sitting by the sea, holding one cold, arthritic hand, I felt as if in her death she was abandoning me unfairly. We talked about my childhood and her youth in a way we could never have done before. It was strangely peaceful. We might have been contemporaries. Yet her account of life in the thirties was as distant to me as gossip from imperial Rome. Sometimes I would glance at her sunken features – the rot still haunted their pallor – and see the outline of my own there, and feel amazed that such a short link connected me to these unimaginable memories. Even my own childhood, when she spoke of it, belonged more to her than to me, until it seemed that I myself – half the evidence for this unexplained person, me – would be carried away into death with her.

Mama (wherever you are), forgive the self-centredness of my feelings then. I did love you. It's just that I'd been destabilised for a time (men, you know) and your going isolated me.

She only touched on her disease once, and that obliquely. In our family it wasn't done to show emotions. Luckily I was watering her potted cyclamens, and had my back turned. She said: "Have you never thought of getting married?"

"Not really. It scares me a bit, you know. It feels too much like prison."

"Not even this . . . Charles, is it?"

"No."

"Well, I suppose you know what you're doing." Her gaze faltered round the sitting-room. "But you know I can't leave you any . . . real security."

My hand touched her shoulder as I passed behind her chair. She understood it. "I'm a doctor, Mama. I don't need security."

"No perhaps not." She rapped with her stick on the floor, as if to steady herself. "All the same."

We didn't talk about it again. After I'd said goodbye to her I felt momentarily torn up and displaced. The thought of her death made me older, lonelier. I suppose you don't really feel adult until your parents have gone.

When I got back to Cruwenath I found a heap of flowers outside my door, with a letter from Daniel. I should have been warmed, but instead I felt oppressed. I remember sitting in my kitchen, downing cups of strong tea, and wondering what the hell to do. If I'd wanted anyone around me then, it would have been Charles, his calm. But I only wanted to be left alone. I plunged back into work next day. Robertson was on holiday and another partner sick, so our clinic was overflowing.

But that evening I was back in the vortex. Daniel looked gaunter from my absence. He'd brought me four or five expensive presents, and waited in suspense for my gratitude. The rest of the evening we spent tangled together on the sofa. Afterwards I found my arms grey with bruises where he'd grasped me. These last times he had moments of losing all gentleness. Once or twice a shared mania gripped us and I'd respond with the same fierceness, swallowed in the whirlpool. Then his tenderness would return in his long cherishing of my mouth and eyes; and the next moment he'd be buried against me. This changeableness unnerved me more and more. Perhaps my mother's fading had reduced my sense of who I was. I don't know. But I became very frightened. I felt as if I was being dragged somewhere – I didn't know where. After he'd gone I'd find myself shaking.

Suddenly I decided to end it.

Even now I'm not sure if I was right. Everything about this man seemed more real, more vivid, than anything else that had happened to me. Yet it was all the product of hopeless delusion. Even while we were walking towards the river that last day – I a little ahead of him – I was telling myself that fantasies faded, that nothing could be built on them.

We spread out our picnic near the old bridge. I felt a dead, cold sadness. I'd worked out several ways of breaking it to him, but now none of them fitted. Yet to talk about anything else, or even to smile at him, seemed hypocrisy. Meanwhile he filled in the silence with small-talk, which sounded even thinner here than it would have indoors. I mentally separated myself from him. I didn't look at him, but at the river. I felt guilty even for eating in front of him. He never touched a thing.

At last his talk faded away in a despairing trickle of jokes. We were left with silence and the river. When I turned back to him his face looked hunted and white. I've seen cancer patients like that. I tried to keep my voice detached, but I felt poised on a diving-board too high for me, not knowing what would happen when I launched off. As I did so, half of me seemed left behind. "Daniel, I just don't think I can take any more. I think you need some other kind of woman. I don't know what kind. But not me . . ."

He refused to accept it. Panic turned his speech to breathy whispers; his eyes looked manic. They frightened me, and increased my will to leave.

His voice was barely audible: "Perhaps we should leave it for a little while."

"I'm going away."

"'Away'?"

"I'm giving up my practice here. I'm going to London." It was only at this moment that I made up my mind to go. When I at last said "I'm leaving you", I felt sick. I stretched out my hand to him in a confusion of sorrow and self-pity. I wanted his forgiveness. He stared at it for a full minute, and once his own hand edged across his knee as if to take it. But he didn't: only went on gazing as if it was a snake or the Holy Grail, and grimaced with pure pain when I withdrew it. I heard myself say: "I can't love you. I want to but I can't." I didn't know if either of these was true.

"Why can't you?"

"I don't know. You frighten me."

"*I* frighten *you*?"

He went on refusing to accept. His dread and pleading walled me off from him now. I was cruelly glad of them. It made everything easier. I thought: I'm right to get away, he's not normal.

"You make me frightened of myself. But I don't want to talk about it. There's no point. I really don't understand it."

"Are you going with Charles?"

"I'm leaving him too."

"How long will you go for?"

Suddenly I felt anger that he was putting us through all this, repeating and repeating the pain. "Understand. *I'm going away for ever.*"

I might have struck him between the eyes. He rocked backwards on his haunches. For a second I saw the idea knocking and battering at his brain. His face convulsed – I had the grotesque fancy that his eyes were going to dangle from their sockets down his cheeks – then it petrified.

"Don't look like that, Daniel. It's not the end of the world."

I gathered our uneaten picnic back into the basket. I was afraid I might weep. My hands were shaking. He sat in the leaves clasping the picnic hamper as if to prevent our going. But at that moment my pity was mainly for myself. I felt as if after all I was leaving the core of me here, in him, and that it was only a husk that was folding up the tablecloth, shaking out the crumbs and walking away.

I heard his footsteps stumbling over the leaves behind me. He called out something, but it was drowned by the noise of the river. I walked on with the tablecloth over my arm. I felt a light fear. His feet came rasping over the bridge's stones. He caught up with me there and I turned towards him. We were both panting although we'd come barely fifty yards. Then, as he stood close, I saw the terror in his face die away. Little by

103

little it was transfigured by a curious surge of calm, a peace so deep and total that it left room for nothing else at all. I think I already knew what he was going to do. But strangely my fear had quite gone, although I love life. I was filled instead by a feeling almost of naturalness, as if I was going to be embraced. As his hand lifted from the hamper its glinting seemed irrelevant. It wasn't like dying at all. I think I even took a step towards him.

Seven

How cold it is here. April already, and the corridors quaking as if sleet were driving through from end to end. It seems weeks since she gave me her story, but it's only four days. It's no good my reading it any more. I can't discover her condition by dissecting her sentences or quite ordinary feelings. But when the weather warms I believe she'll return to the garden (she loved gardens) or sit in the pavilions under the trees, like the other patients do. The crocuses have gone now, and lakes of daffodils are glowing under the outer wall. For all I know she's been here years and I haven't noticed, while the nails were being driven into her mind's coffin.

There's an ugliness in this ward too. It's splitting into camps. One of the charge nurses is on sick leave and his place has been taken by a simpering staff nurse who spends most of her time in the glass office reading magazines or telephoning her boyfriend. Then there's nobody to defuse the tension. The Boss and his poker-players sit on orange plastic chairs in the dining-area. They crouch over their table in layers of cigarette smoke while money flickers between them, usually in the direction of the Boss. His breast pockets bulge and his trousers jangle with coins whenever he shifts his buttocks. Sometimes they all seem to be in conference: Boss, Prick, a sad-faced ex-roadmender and a shipping clerk. The Boss says: "Watcha got in your hand, Prick?" He stares at him with his screwdriver eyes. But Prick is impenetrable: not like Gregory. Prick just sits there, thumbing his deck with one hand and scratching his chest with the other. It's no good anyone trying to thought-read him, because there's nothing to read. But the cards are so soiled and tattered that I reckon the Boss knows the back of each one anyway.

Orgill and Evans are painting the dormitory blue, and sometimes Sheldon joins them, working his brush with supple-wristed strokes, as if still sawing that noiseless violin. Half-smoked cigarettes pass from Orgill to Evans and some-times to Sheldon, ending at Buddha who never hands them on, but just lies flat out on his bed, reading or looking at the ceiling. The floors are littered with ash and the walls are still parti-coloured. Orgill gets bored. He'll suddenly rush out to do something he's forgotten in O.T. or the community hall. Or he'll bounce down on Buddha's bed and join in whatever he's reading – the *Bhagavad Gita* or Karen Horney's *Self-Analysis* – exclaiming every few seconds "Isn't it beautiful!" or "Wow, this guy knew a thing!" The next moment he's saying: "Hey, boys, how about a visit to the Chronics?" or "Want a cuppa in the Social, lads?" and they all troop out.

It's when everyone gathers in the television room that the trouble starts.

"How the fuck long are we having skewbald walls in the dorm?" The Boss's pipe raps its alarum on his armchair. "We all going to lie there inhaling paint fumes for the next five years, huh?"

"Don't you bug yourself, Boss. It'll be done. Tomorrow, maybe day after. Besides, it's therapeutic." Orgill swirls the sounds in his mouth. "Yessir. Ther-ah-poo-tick. Come to think of it, this lounge could take a gloss too."

"You lay a paint-brush on here," the Boss says, "and I'll crack yer skull in. Anyways, that sort of thing gets decided in Patients' Council. You can't frick about painting every goddam thing in sight."

"But look at it!" Orgill waves his hands at the walls. "Some kind of maroon gunk. No wonder everyone's depressed in here. Let's do it in sky-blue."

"Your favourite colour, I'll bet," the Boss says. "Baby blue."

"God, Boss, you're so *old*." Orgill tosses his yellow mane. "I reckon some of you guys just *want* to be gloomy. You're revelling in it. D'you know, I haven't heard *one laugh* since I came into this ward. *Not a single laugh*."

"Jesus wept." The Boss wrenches his tie loose as if he can't breathe. "Laugh! What's there to *laugh* about here? The only ones who *laugh* here are the Chronics. If you laugh it means you're a fucking screwball. They'll put you up in Disturbed. So just quit wanking, Orgill. Get yer specs on."

". . . Not so much as a chuckle or a compliment," Orgill is going on. "Not even a smile. Nothing. Look, Boss." He crouches on his haunches to focus the man's face. "I've met some great people in this place, I can tell you. It can't be a bad dump if there's blokes like Evans and Sheldon in it. Don't you see? It's . . ."

The nurse's voice comes over the microphone: "Not too much noise, please, Mr Orgill [it's always him] there are patients trying to watch the television."

But nobody takes much notice of her. (She wears short skirts under her regulation blue uniform, ready to make off for the evening.) Orgill is still crouched by the Boss.

". . . All you gotta do is find where *it* is, Boss. It's always there, waiting." His soft grey eyes press and gleam into the other's scrunched-up pits. "Honestly, I look at you and I can't bear to see a man so bloody miserable."

The Boss's head is shaking slightly. His voice comes gravelly. "You're right up the pissing wall, Orgill. Evans' got a few holes in the nut but you're a Gorgonzola."

But Orgill is still pressing him. Each pink hand is locked on an arm of the Boss's chair. "You don't see at all, do you? You just don't see." He breathes out intensely: "*Take a new look. See the glory, see the holiness!*"

The Boss explodes. "Are you some pukey kind of Christian?"

"Sure I'm Christian . . ."

"Then what about original sin and shit, huh? And what's that Buddhist pseud doing with you? What's . . ."

"Gentlemen," the microphone crackles "a little less noise, please."

"Look, man." Orgill's face is close to the Boss's again. You'd think he was going to kiss him. "Buddha, Christ, you, me, him – what's the difference? That's not where it's at." He aches for the Boss to realise, to have faith in whatever it is. "I love you, man."

Then he stands up, runs his fingers irritably through his hair, and lopes away into the dormitory with his disciples.

I was sitting next to the Boss, and saw his fists thumping and grinding on the arms of his chair long after Orgill had gone. And his head continued shaking, while sweaty locks of red-grey hair splashed round his face. I didn't know whether this was anger or something else. Perhaps he didn't either.

He noticed me watching him and muttered: "*He*'s trying to tell *me* what the world's like. When I was down the pit, he was in his diapers."

"He's no harm."

"Harm?" The Boss seemed to have lost his voice. It grated and whispered. "But he don't respect the fucking *truth*, Prof., that's what I can't take. He's just fooling himself. And those other poor bastards too, Sheldon and Evans and the fat contemplator. They're great, he says, but he must know they're as much use as a spare prick at a wedding." He was talking as much to himself as to me, as if Orgill were inside him and he were trying to kick him out. "Orgill wants to paint the whole world sky-blue, and he can't even see under his nose. All the time he was talking, that nurse was on to her buzzers and recorders. Doesn't he know the whole ward's bugged? But he goes crapping on like that."

"We're not bugged here, Boss."

His face wrenched towards me. I couldn't see his eyes at all. They were drowned in a surge of clenching cheeks and brows. "'Course we are, Prof. Christ. There's one right here" – he dug a finger at the floor under his chair – "and another up

108

there" – he pitched his jaw at the ceiling. "They've got us netted every which way. You can't breathe."

Through the glass-panelled dormitory door I noticed Orgill's group engaged in some ceremony. They were seated on stools around one of the beds, with books and a cassette tape recorder. Their eyes were closed and their hands rested palms upward on the bed.

"What the hell's he got them doing now?" said the Boss.

Buddha kept lifting and quivering one hand in a characteristic gesture of pacification. Orgill sat with his back to us. I saw him reach out and adjust the cassette recorder, then heard the ageless shimmer of sitar music. Beneath the cacophony of a television Western it trembled faintly, persistently, into the ward – a sinuous tendril without end or beginning. Even now Orgill's gang were circulating half-smoked cigarettes, then they closed their eyes again while those hypnotic noises wove around them – sounds in which intricacy and enormousness were one, and the individual merely a grace-note in the long continuum of life, a shimmer upwards or a feint downwards, no more, as if man were a wave on the sea of God.

"They're barmy," said the Boss.

"They're praying."

He rapped his pipe. "But it's too easy, isn't it, Prof? The motherfuckers. They fart and it's God." He iterated slowly: "Mum-bo Jum-bo."

I wasn't surprised to find Gregory in the library. Sometimes the air in Faraday ward stiffens into something viscid. You have to push through it, batter, shout to be heard, it swims so thick. But the library air is only a thin, golden dust. It smells of calmness and crumbled leather. It's autumn here, whatever the season outside. There's an old record-player and a heap of monophone discs. Bach, Haydn, Mozart, Beethoven, Berlioz. The room seems full of rotting fruit.

Gregory was sitting on the window-sill. He looked as old and completed as the books. Since his breakdown a few days before, the skin over his cheekbones shone so taut and glassy that you expected it to splinter apart if he so much as sucked in his lips, and his eyes lurked in black-rimmed sockets. I felt nervously sad for him. He usually keeps his troubles to himself. Only in the last week he'd suddenly unbent and scattered this desperation round him. At first I thought it a new strength that he could talk to me. But I was wrong. His head looks scarcely balanced on his neck now. It's more like a balloon on a string. I sat by him on the sill. Even the light looked ancient.

"I couldn't stay up in the ward," he said. "It makes me feel I'm going over the border. To see four grown men sitting round a bed . . . and the Boss like a bloodhound . . . oh no . . . no . . . We're headed for something bad up there."

I'd felt the same. As if something were rocking. But I didn't say so. "The Boss shouldn't be there much longer. He must be ready for discharge."

"You're just saying that, Daniel. But he won't go yet . . . perhaps not ever. He's a severe schizophrenic, even I can tell. Perhaps that's why he can look inside people."

"I don't know about this looking inside." But I'd felt what he meant. The Boss exerts a pressure, a forcefield. Maybe we all do, I don't know, maybe Gregory's and mine are just weak.

"Oh he does look, he does" – Gregory's hands started their writhing – "even though you often can't see his eyes at all. That's because they're scouring inside your head. It doesn't sound true, I realise that, but when it happens you know it. Things aren't right up there, Daniel. It's the first time in years I've felt I might leave . . . just discharge myself."

"*Discharge* yourself? Can you?"

"Oh yes." He smiled rather sheepishly. "You see, I was never legally committed. It's rather hard to say this . . ." he clamped his hands under his armpits. "I'd be prouder to have been committed. There's something cowardly about doing it oneself . . . do you think? Usually I think that."

I've known him all these years, I thought, and I never realised.

He wouldn't look at me. He was staring at the floor. "But I did it to protect others, you see . . . to protect them from me. There are things in me that can't be cured, terrible things.

110

Maybe it's punishment and people become as they deserve. But then I look at Evans and think: why is *he* here? He's so young. All that whimpering at night. It's so confusing, Daniel. One moment I'm thinking this, then I'll think the opposite. But at least I'm not out there, not damaging anyone else . . ."

"Look here, Gregory, you wouldn't hurt a fly. What in God's name are you talking about?" But this robust tone sounded false between us.

Gregory's shoulders convulsed slightly, his hands still locked beneath them. He said: "Don't you ever find something just comes up out of you . . . that you didn't know about? Suddenly it's just there. Something very strong . . . too strong.".

I hunted for what I'd say, and of course I found Sophia. "Yes, for women. I feel that about women."

He rocked a little. "That's what I mean. Sex."

I waited, but he was silent. He wanted a return confidence. I said: "In my case there's this trouble about my mother. I must have told you. I'm an analyst's field-day. I lost my mother when I was eight."

He sent me a havering smile. "Was she like you?"

"I think so." My voice went foolishly casual. "Half Jewish. A bit barmy. Wrote poetry and stuff."

Once I showed my own poetry to her. Like an idiot. She looks at it and stares back blankly. Piercing blue eyes. Empty. My father says: "There, there, old boy, she's just having one of her turns." Christ.

I said: "But why this protecting the world from yourself? You're not Jack the Ripper." But he looked so wretched that I regretted saying it.

"It's as I say . . . I suppose you'd call it sex, yes. . . ." He was rocking up and down unbearably, still gazing at the floor. His shadow there was even thinner than he was. "That's why it was right to be shut up here. You see, it's the only place where . . . where *there aren't any children*."

I hadn't anticipated that. "But it must have been years ago, Gregory, when you did whatever it was."

"No. I'd been here for years before I actually . . . did it. But in some ways it wasn't quite my fault, it really wasn't, Daniel.

111

I didn't seek it." He spoke in a rush, as if I were accusing him. "It was when I was assigned to the rehabilitation home in Swansea. I was just sitting in the bus and she comes and sits beside me . . . right beside me in an empty bus. She had these auburn curls. She can't have been more than ten years old, and she was reading her book with these dark eyes, huge and black under beautiful lashes . . . and then, then I don't know what made me do it, Daniel, it's as I was saying it just . . . but my hand was on her thigh." He suddenly clasped his head. "Yet I can't remember the hand going there, only that it was there. . . ." His bent arms hid his face. " . . . And she looks at me. I can't describe her expression. A sort of dovelike horror. I see myself suddenly too, this atrocious, ancient thing, this thing with its claw on her . . . my face like something . . . and me the age of her grandfather."

"Then what?"

"She goes to the farthest seat as if I was a leper."

"And then?"

"Isn't that *enough*? What comes after that?" He peered at me as if I might be joking. "In a minute I'd . . . I'd be loitering round the latrines in children's playgrounds. I'd. . . ." His hands unleashed, clenched his thighs. "I think that's why I can't stand to look at Orgill. There's a kind of idiot goodness about him, isn't there? He could see inside me too, if he wanted. Tell me honestly . . . honestly, Daniel . . . do I smell?"

"*What?*"

"Do I smell? Because that's what's inside, you know. That's what's really inside. Dung. I'm made of faeces. Can't you smell?"

God, he's going right round the bend.

"Stop it, Gregory, stop it." My own voice was quaking. My hands too. I stuffed them in my pockets. I'd met this kind of thing among the Chronics. One of them – a near-cripple – would only eat with a plastic knife, he was so afraid of murdering. This violated angel-child of Gregory's was probably some smutty high school kid who'd gone back and joked with her classmates how some old boy touched her up as if she were the B.V.M. But *he* was back in a mental hospital.

112

Not that it could be her fault, it was just the way he was. We're all cursed in this place.

Afterwards I went out and looked for Sophia. I could have followed the way blindfold – into the Social room which was crowded only by men, snooping round the Occupational Therapy galleries, peering into the sewing-room which was always empty, lingering round the iron doors in case they opened, across to the community hall dotted with men in wheelchairs and aged female Chronics sipping tea, chirruping to nothing, burning their fingers on the plastic mugs, sleeping. This search reeked of futility now. She was never there. And if she had been, what would we have done or said?

It was early the next evening, for the first time, that I found the doors ajar. Beyond them the dormitory was empty, just a mortuary of vacant beds. Even to peer inside it set me trembling. The place held a kind of desolate promise. I padded to the dormitory's end and turned as I had once seen her turn, into a passage leading to another curtained door. I listened outside it. The voice of a television newscaster was announcing an air crash, and through the door's crack, eased open by my foot, appeared a vacant semicircle of women's faces, gazing.

I heard a sharp intake of breath. "What are you doing in here?" An assistant nurse was standing behind me, furious.

"Look, I'm . . ."

"Get out! Out, out!" Her voice went shrill. She advanced on me, five-foot-nothing in her green uniform, and half pushed me back down the passage, back through the dormitory between the sepulchral beds, towards the outer door.

"Listen, nurse . . . I'm a voluntary worker on Faraday . . . I'm trying to . . ."

"Don't tell me things." She pulled the iron door wide behind me. "Just get back where you belong!" It clanged to.

And there I am, propped in the corridor, feeling sick (and a male Chronic peeing on the tiled wall five feet away). And I recognise this as a special kind of nightmare: the kind only I get in. It's familiar. I'm back in my old love–fear. I never really left it. While she, of course, is invulnerable as ever, sitting in the ward in a television daze (although I hadn't seen her), oblivious of me, of anything. It was I who was by the precipice. Just as it always used to be.

After a minute I pulled myself together, went back to Faraday and tried to work out a scheme. I had to discover her diagnosis. Perhaps she was suffering from some incurable type of personality disorder. Maybe she'd even been wrongly diagnosed. I'd heard of women patients, 'borderlines' as they were called, who turned out not to be schizophrenic at all but merely hysterical. They assimilated and copied the disorders of the patients around them. They feigned madness, produced symptoms to order. The way to help her would simply be to understand her, instead of pumping her with drugs.

As I got into the ward, a chaos of different plans – ruminated, deferred and reconsidered over the past days – at last coalesced. They centred on the glass office which overlooked the dormitory on one side, the television room on the other. At the moment it was locked, and a charge nurse was in the sitting-room with some of the patients. But in a little while, when the night shift came on, the young staff nurse would be there instead, reading her magazines.

I found Gregory dozing in the dormitory. I sat on his bed. I didn't want to alarm him, but I couldn't delay any longer. "Gregory, I've got a favour to ask you. You're the only one I can trust."

He blinked at me and swivelled his feet to the ground. We sat side by side on his bed like scheming schoolboys. Only a soft light penetrated through the panelled door. He already sounded nervous: "What is it?"

"You know this woman I've been worried about, the one who was in the church the other day? Well, she's someone I used to know."

"Used to know, Daniel? How can that be?"

"A long time ago." I couldn't tell, in the gloom, how frightened his eyes were, sunk in their caves. "I need to get her diagnosis."

114

"That's impossible . . . you can't. They never let them out."

"But I *have* to, Gregory. She may be curable. I *have* to." I couldn't make out his expression in the dark, but focused my hope on the sad blob of his head.

"What could *you* do?"

"I don't know. But I can't do anything until I know what's wrong."

We were silent for a full minute. I waited while the facts worked their way into him. He began looking at me cautiously, sitting on his hands, wondering. At last he said: "What do you want me to do?"

"It'll be very simple. All I need is to get into that office behind us. They keep a general list on the whole hospital, photocopied from Administration. I know because one of the nurses told me. The list has a breakdown on every patient in the place – name, ward, diagnosis, date of admission. I just want five minutes in there to find it. *Five minutes.*" I paused. He didn't say a thing. "What I need is someone to create a diversion to get the nurse out."

"Oh no." He shook his head. "You can't . . . you can't do that sort of thing. No . . . oh no . . . no. . . ."

I suppressed a surge of resentment. Simply to have voiced the possibility seemed to have brought it nearer. I said: "Look, Gregory. All you've got to do is suddenly pretend sickness in the T.V. sitting-room. Just slip off your chair on to the floor. That'll bring her out."

"She'd lock the office door behind her, Daniel. They always do."

"Not if you do it suddenly enough, no, and not this staff nurse. She won't."

He shook his head again. "I'm sorry, I couldn't. I just couldn't. I'm sorry. Ask one of the others."

"How can I? Sheldon and Evans would be too frightened. Orgill would want to know all about it and can't keep a thing to himself, and I can't trust the rest." I waited again, and he was silent again. I grimaced at the white blob in the dark. It seemed such a frail thing for my hopes to break on. As his silence prolonged I felt a tremor of panic. I said cruelly: "If you refuse, you may be condemning somebody to madness. Have you ever been inside a Chronics' ward? If you think this ward's bad . . ." *Don't make me visualise these things.*

He said: "But if they think I'm ill they'll want to treat me. They'll think I'm going down again." He let out a harrowed moan. "They could even try electro-convulsive."

Then I knew it was hopeless.

Damn you. But I said nothing. I just left, barged out through the doorway. I felt on the brink of something violent. I couldn't stand the television room. They were almost all there. I went into the kitchen and sank down on a stool and closed my eyes. Prick was on the washing-up rota, and I just listened to him crashing the knives and plates over the draining-board as if they were crashing in my head.

For all I knew Sophia didn't even want to come back from wherever she was. After all, she was still in control – of me, of her. Sitting by the television, quite contained. Keeping herself a void. No pain, no exposure. Nothing. Just staring at the rectangle of other people's lives.

"What's bugging you, Prof?"

It was Prick, looking down at me, cleaning his neck with the drying-up cloth. He'd only been in the ward a few weeks, and I didn't know him at all. Perhaps it was this, or my desperation, or just his skittle-shaped body, which made me say: "Will you roll over in a faint for ten quid?"

His mouth hung slightly open. "Nope."

"I mean *pretend*."

"I've got my reputation to think of. I don't faint."

Little clumps of hair stuck up from his head at all angles, tufted his ears and spurted from his nostrils.

I said: "Well just be sick then. Lie on the floor. Anything. But keep the nurse engaged for five minutes."

I took out my wallet and riffled through some notes.

Prick looked at them with the closest I'd seen to expression. He ran his tongue round his mouth. "I'll do you a lie-down job for ten, Prof., or a faint for twenty." He stuck out his hand. "Gimme fifty and I'll jump out the window. Heh."

"Do me a faint, then. At nine-thirty. And keep her engaged

for at least five minutes." I dropped two tenners into the work-scarred palm.

He said: "What'll I tell Boss?"

"Tell him you did it for a bet."

He rammed the notes into his back trouser pocket. "If I get the kiss of life from her, Prof., you get a refund." He threw the drying-up cloth into the sink, then stopped in the doorway. "Say, Prof. . . ."

"Yes."

"What's the game, huh?"

"It's a gag."

"Right," he said, and went out.

It was nearly nine o'clock already. I went into the television room where the charge nurse was administering drugs before he finished shift. Then I wandered into the dormitory. There was nobody there. I lay down on the bed nearest the darkened office, unstrapped my watch and placed it by the pillow. Then I arranged myself shapelessly under a blanket, and ruffled it over my head until the office was framed under a loose fold. Then I waited.

A minute after nine o'clock the staff nurse settled in the glass cube like a goldfish in an illuminated tank. The noise of the television sounded faint through the walls. For a while she sat filling in forms at the desk, then stood up, emerged languidly and locked the door behind her. Light and noise spilled into the dormitory as she opened the sitting-room door, then they died.

It was nine-fifteen. I waited for her to return. By the time she did so ten minutes later, I was oozing sweat under the blanket. A few inches from my face the second-hand of the watch trembled round its golden digits with a cold-blooded life of its own. Its ticking thundered in the silence. In the office the nurse's shape looked exotic and lonely, its face lowered in shadow. The pages turning in her hands sent out a brittle, faraway slapping.

Nine-thirty, and I watched her. My breathing had nearly stopped. There was no sound from next door. The blanket formed a black tunnel round my head. At its end she sat

117

absolutely still, embalmed in her gold-lit cube. The watch-hand juddered on. Five minutes on. She turned a page. My breathing deepened into hot, heavy sighs. My legs were going numb. The watch-face became the utterance of my misery as the minutes poured on. For a while it had seemed to hold its motion still, poised, but now it was turning faster and faster. The nurse was turning the pages faster too. The light in her aquarium looked brighter. Time was speeding up, running away from me.

I was a fool to give him the money first, of course. He must be laughing, watching that damn television. And Sophia watching it too, perfectly content, somewhere else. And only I in this craze of love-fear, anointed in sweat, my whole body numb. And nearly ten o'clock. Even the minute-hand was flying, the hour-hand lumbering after it. He'd just say "Gotcha that time didn't I, Prof?" Little bastard. And she sickening into dust.

Like a marionette in stage-light, the nurse jerked up. Something thrashed and moaned next door. For a second she flickered across her illumined tank, then, with what seemed one continuous motion, she opened both doors, letting in a spurt of noise, and vanished.

The lamp in the office was still on, and its door swinging. I dropped my legs to the floor, wondering if they'd hold me. Then I bolted in, bent double. Two drawers of files. I could hardly pull them out, I was shaking so violently. They were stuffed full. My fingers slithered and trembled over them. 'Patients', 'Finance', 'Medication', 'Group Therapy'. Through the glass partition behind me I glimpsed the television room in dumb-show – a single square hand lifted above the crouched shoulders of the nurse on the floor. My fingers darted to the front of the drawer, fumbled into its centre. Even my shoulders shook. 'Industrial Therapy', 'Visitors', 'Director of Nursing'. My hand closed on 'Admin. General'. The file spilt onto the floor. I went on hands and knees, scrabbling among the papers, and saw in the desk's shadow: 'General List'. It was thick and rough. Even in my fingers, which had frozen, its pages turned. I held it on my lap. The women were at the back, in alphabetical order. There were seven or eight entries to a page. I was pierced and shaken with cold. The names and dates and diagnoses juddered on my knees. 'Auditory hallucinosis', 'Catatonic schizophrenia', 'Psychopathic personality', 'Obsessional neurosis'. Adams, Allen, Benson, Bryfdir, Carson . . . I clamped them on the floor, hunted for Brown. I leafed through all sixty patients, thinking she must have been misplaced.

But she wasn't there at all.

Gently, ruminatively almost, I flickered back through the pages as if I might have missed her, then gathered up the documents and slid them into the file. When I stood up I realised with a distant surprise that I'd stopped shaking now and instead was heavy as wood, barely able to move coherently at all, let alone fast. I returned 'Admin. General' to its place, and closed the drawer. I was standing upright, fully visible in the glass box, but nobody saw me. In the sitting-room Prick was slumped in a chair, but smiling to himself, and the poor girl half kneeling in front of him. It reminded me, for some reason, of a Bible illumination.

There seemed nothing more to do. Hopelessly I pulled out the other drawer, but it contained only the files of the Faraday patients: Sheldon, Morgan, Nisbet, Orgill, Pashley . . .

Pashley. I dipped a hand tiredly into mine (because I am a patient), and found my admission form. It was covered in little squares with ticks or lines through them. Against 'Diagnosis' I read '*Chronic dissociative state. Depersonalisation syndrome.*' The space for my previous admissions was crammed with dates and the names of rehabilitation homes and sheltered accommodation. When I saw it like that, it looked unutterably depressing. I picked out my other papers, with a progress report from the unit psychiatrist. I read at random: '*The patient composes cathartic stories showing his usual inability to distinguish between fact and fantasy. These seem partly wish-fulfilment, and partly quite sophisticated attempts to come to terms with a real or imagined loss.*'

Then I found a note dated only yesterday, from the psychiatrist to the charge nurses: '*Pashley is showing symptoms of impending relapse. Will probably peak in ten to twelve days. I have amended his drug regimen. Keep me informed.'*

Well, it's always interesting to know what they think.

It's still not a lie that I'm a worker here. They let me run the essay competition, and the unit psychiatrist says he's found the results helpful.

Unfortunately it's true that I composed Sophia's story myself. I can only say that it was intended as an effort to understand her, to sympathise with how she must have thought and felt. In this sense, at least, it may have approached the truth. If I portrayed her as unattractive, that is how she saw herself. Or perhaps I wanted to hold her a little away from me. I don't know. But the memory of her beauty is intolerable now.

Eight

It's coming.

Even an outsider could sense it. Orgill has this dangerous charisma. They're in the dormitory most afternoons, he and Sheldon, Evans, Buddha. He attacks the walls in ferocious bouts, cutting great swathes of blue across them with a foot-wide brush. The paint dribbles down to the skirting and smoothes over the floor in thick pools. Sheldon and Evans follow him holding narrower brushes, filling in the gaps with frail dabs. The wrenched-up shoulders of the one, and the quivering arms of the other, look ethereal against the sky-blue.

Sooner or later they'll gather for their ceremony (or whatever it is), but a little to one side of the door panel now, so they're not so easily glimpsed. The staff don't interfere with them; they think it's group therapy. But Orgill's like a wild Christ. His bed becomes a tabernacle. They sit round its empty white-ness, palms cupped, bathed in the sitar music. Sometimes Buddha reads something aloud. And all the time Orgill presides at the top of the bed, shaking his great head of flax and burning them up with his eyes.

The Boss is out of sight, of course. They've taken to playing canasta in the dining-area now, and you can feel the fumes of repressed temper around them. When money changes hands, it often goes to the shipping clerk. The Boss grinds him with stares, and after they've toted up the score he'll ask: "How d'you work it then? You hold back on your wild cards? Or can you memorise what we blokes pick up off the discard pile?" Then he'll absorb the answers and go quiet for a bit, half smiling at the clerk and nodding pensively in something like admiration. He respects that sort of cleverness.

But most of the time they play in near-silence. The Boss reverts to poker and wins back what he lost. They lean forward all together, their forearms splayed over the little table and their heads almost touching so you'd think they cribbed each other's hands. Sometimes they seem conflated into a single, simmering blackness. The gloom of the dining-area must have something to do with this (we're meant to conserve electricity and not use the strip-lights) together with the drabness of their jackets. When at last they put the cards away they remain muttering together for a while, and you wonder what they can be talking about. They're impenetrable. They might be sitting in a dockside café instead of here. They make Orgill's crew seem pale as blancmange.

The sitting-room is a no-man's land, peopled by the rest of us. Many sit along the walls in tiredness or withdrawal. But yesterday afternoon the room became a battlefield for the television. The Boss wanted to watch a boxing match, but Orgill opted for a Marilyn Monroe film. Behind each of them murmured their supporters.

The Boss sat in his favourite chair before the still-blank screen. His tie was dragged loose around his open-necked shirt so you could see where the red neck thickened into his shoulders, lapped by rusty hairs. "So you think I'm giving up the world welterweight champ for some ancient movie, huh?"

Orgill was grinning. "It's a great movie, Boss. Funny as hell. It'll split your sides. Do you good." He was sitting cross-legged on the floor, balancing his sneakered feet on his fists.

"I don't want my sides split, Orgill. I want to see the two best scrappers in the business."

Orgill jumped to his feet. "Okay lads, then, we'll put it to the vote!"

122

"The hell with that." The Boss got up and switched the television to his channel, then lumbered back to his seat.

"Please no, Boss. This is *democracy*. We got seventeen other guys in this ward." Orgill spread out his arms to the man with an expression of extraordinary pain. Sometimes he looks at him like a disappointed father. It's strange. You can see he wants to do something about him, as if he might recreate him, resurrect him. His soft, pink hands beat together in frustration. He doesn't feel threatened at all: just sad and bemused. He gave a sigh, then stared round him and demanded: "Who wants to look at Marilyn Monroe? You can go to Wembley any time once you're out, but you can't see this . . ."

"You're wrong there, Orgill," said the shipping clerk. "They revive these old films all the time."

"Not this one they don't." Orgill crouched down in front of a row of other patients and swept them back and forth with his eyes. "C'mon fellows. D'you want to fall about in love and laughter, or see two guys mashing one another? It's a straight choice! Beauty or the Beast?"

But they were either without courage or without opinion. None of them ventured a word. Gregory and I were joining an outing organised by the women's wards, and we didn't vote either. We got up to go.

"A straight choice my arse," the Boss said. His mouth showed little vixen's teeth, which looked too small for it. "That's not love you're after, Orgill, that's sex. And as for laughter, your jackass cackling would have gone on in Belsen. It's just a *laughing gas* reaction, Orgill. Ever heard of that?"

Sometimes I get confused, and wonder whether it isn't Orgill, after all, who's a kind of deluding anti–Christ, and whether the Boss, in his bitter way, is not better than he seems. It's impossible to know, because neither of them leaves you alone. The Boss, in particular, is like a bulldog. Once he gets you by the neck he never lets off, but goes on scruffing and munching closer to the larynx until he can shake you like a kitten. And sometimes I think: that's right, that's the truth, that's what we deserve. That's why Gregory never confronts him. Nor I. He can just shake us, make us feel it's true.

Yet Orgill escapes, effortlessly, automatically, simply by being what he is. It's inexplicable.

Gregory and I went down the stairs in silence to Inner Reception. Our two coaches, when they arrived, were already full of female Chronics collected from another entrance, and we were ushered into the second of them with some other men. But before we left I walked quickly round the first coach and suddenly caught a glimpse of Sophia sitting farthest from the window, her profile absolutely still beyond her neighbour's. As we crunched down the yellow drive, mounded with its rhododendrons, I could see the back of her brown head jostled among the white and greying ones.

Then the coaches separated and we were winding alone past ramshackle farmhouses and cottages, following one of those rock-scattered streams up through a valley to the ruins of a medieval priory. The beauty and release of this were almost painful. I simply stared out of the window at the chalk-white lambs in the fields, at the different flocks of sheep sprayed with their owners' blue or ochre dyes, at the glaze of new green over the hills. Sophia's coach was out of sight. Even now, for all I knew, she might be disembarking at the priory ruins. And I told myself that when I saw her I'd persist with a single question: 'What is your new name?'

Because only after I'd closed up the files in that glass office had it dawned on me. Ten years is a long time. Why had I searched for her under 'Brown'? Of course, she'd been married.

I was filled with an odd peace. I went on staring out, while the hills poured in. Along the valley thin lines of hazel quartered the slopes into pastureland, and eroded rain-paths split them through the scrub. They lifted to heights too steep even for the Welsh mountain sheep – hill-crests patterned with enigmatic tracks, very straight, like fire-breaks for forests now vanished. The priory rose near the head of a naked valley. The ancient woods had gone, which once (said a Saxon chronicler) touched the heavens.

By the time we arrived the others were already inside the

ruins. A cold wind rattled in and out. A single shattered aisle rose from the sward, crowned by close-set clerestory windows, mostly broken. Gregory and I wandered beneath them, staring up to where the lopped sheafs of fan vaulting were reduced to graceless spurts of stone. We hunted for the few Gothic details left, while I watched out for her. I avoided seeming to seek her. I hoped she might even approach me. The female Chronics dithered and whispered and fidgeted with their handbags, and occasionally settled in the remaining aisle to gaze up without expression at that enormous certainty of stone.

It was a long time before I saw her. She was standing some way away in the vaulted shadow of the slype, the one ruin still covered. I waited but she didn't move, only stood there in an old duffle coat and slacks, quite alone, apparently looking at nothing. As I got to my feet she turned away and began to retrace her steps, exactly as if she'd seen me. I circled into the transept from the other direction, and waited where its windows threw thirty-foot shadows into the ruins. After a minute I heard a woman talking to herself: "I don't have to stay, you know . . . they'll come and take me any time I want . . . I only have to say . . . I don't have to stay, you know . . ." She comes nearer. A weird acoustic in the ruins. I can't decide if it's Sophia, her voice is so changed now. It slithers and jangles among the stones. Then it stops and I see nobody.

I walk deeper into the transept under the disheartening spring of those vaults, like broken rockets. The walls are criss-crossed in shadows. You'd think they moved. Some of the stones are hewn smooth, others left jagged. The next moment, in the gap between two buttresses, she's there.

She stares at me, then turns on her heel and vanishes. I gaze back at the place where she'd stood. She doesn't return, and I'm holding my stomach as if I'd been kicked (perhaps it's the cold). I run round to the chapter-house. Everybody coming this way has to pass through it. (How have I failed her?) But of course she knows I'm there. I hear her feet crunching in its roofless apse. The long, springy step. It turns and stops. Then goes away.

125

And suddenly the ruins are coughing up water. It erupts between the futile start of arches in the air, I can't stop it, it retches in spasms out of my lungs, heart, chest, throat into my tight-shut eyes, where it falls in a disfiguring mass of tears inside my anorak and onto the grey-red stones. It seems centred in my stomach. I bend double against the wall to stop it. But of course it's only emptiness in there. I wonder why I'm not spitting blood. Or falling.

Gregory approaches me anxiously. I turn away from him because I don't know how to explain. As he passes he lays a hand gently on my forearm, as if he were touching it casually, going by. For a while I hear his footsteps soft and agitated over the grass behind me, until he comes and says: "Danny, we're going back now."

These Patients' Councils are supposed to motivate and give us confidence. It is now that we air our grievances with the staff, the system and one another (but the staff and the system get off lightly). We sit round one of the tables in Occupational Therapy with the unit psychiatrist. On the walls our paintings betray us with a circle of bleak or bitter presences.

This evening our elected chairman was the sad-faced road-mender, who was out of his depth. The only real authority, of course, belonged to the psychiatrist. This man has the absolute power to discharge or detain us, and while the patients are apparently talking to one another, they are really appealing to him. He sits democratically in the thick of us – a big man with a bland, Humpty-Dumpty expression. He sometimes looks amused in a distant way. He's been trained into a wary benignity. But he doesn't belong to us. You can't imagine such a face weeping or falling in love.

People become unnaturally polite at these councils. The Boss seems physically to reduce in size, and addresses the psychiatrist with a dogged deference. His lower lip starts to hang loose, and he even smiles a little. The older or more withdrawn of us hover on the fringes of the rest, and sometimes seem on the point of drifting away altogether. Only Orgill carries on just the same, roistering and chattering and suggesting bizarre schemes for group therapy which never develop. His acolytes circle him like dead planets, while the Boss and friends confront them across the table. They're split as fiercely as that now.

This evening the Boss did little but loom forward in his chair sucking his charred pipe in a watchful temper. It was obvious who'd won the television battle. There was a desultory discussion about smoking in the dormitory, but you could tell the complainant wasn't really attacking the culprit, only saying: "Look, shrink, let me out of this filthy place, I'm too good for it." Somebody moaned about Orgill cooking snacks at all hours, and somebody else grumbled at the way the shower-taps were left dripping at night, "so you can't hear yourself sleeping." But the psychiatrist rarely interferes. We're meant to solve our own problems. He just looks on through his button eyes. You have the suspicion he's not precisely seeing human beings at all, but is observing a conflux of interesting or predictable symptoms playing games with one another (and with him.) I wonder how I'm meant to act. I just look at them through the fog of my wretchedness as if I weren't in this ward at all but only a visitor, listening in. I suppose I'm behaving with typical *chronic dissociation*, whatever that is. But if I didn't I'd only be rediagnosed as a something else. You can't escape. So I just settle down and think of Sophia until my eyes glaze over and my stomach starts its thudding and disgorging. It's as if there's a drum being pounded in there, and the thuds shoot up high inside my chest under where the collar-bones meet, then freeze.

I come round to hear Buddha talking in a high voice, which seems to have struggled out from far inside his fatness and arrived depleted. His coat lapels have sprouted nuclear disarmament badges. He's saying: ". . . So half the dorm beds aren't made up at all, I don't know who's organising the rota this week . . ."

"I've been *trying* to," says the shipping clerk, "but I have to say that making up the beds isn't always a pleasant task." He stops, as if everybody must get his drift of meaning.

Prick says: "Yup. I just can't be making all those beds. I can't be making Sheldon's"

Sheldon jumps.

Prick continues as if he wasn't there. "He goes to bed in his day-clothes, that's the trouble. I think he pisses in them in the day. Makes the bed smell rotten."

Sheldon has almost withered away. His head is hanging horizontal to the table and his fiddle-arm is juddering back and forth pathetically as if he were trying to scratch his chest.

Orgill plunges in before the psychiatrist. "I think you're hallucinating, man!" He puts his arms round Sheldon's shoulders, which quake inside them. He stares at Prick. "Yeah. You're just sniffing one of your gang. Wouldn't *I* know if Charlie here smelt? We're together all day. Since when did you even *talk* to him?" He tries to peer into Sheldon's face. "You don't smell do you, Charlie? No, he never smelt in his life, and that's it."

The Boss says with sinister courtesy: "I think Mr Orgill maybe don't smell Mr Sheldon because they're always painting together. That paint'd outsmell anything. In my humble opinion, Mr Sheldon shouldn't sleep in his day-clothes. After all" – he looks at Orgill – "there's seventeen other guys in this ward, and the rest of us can't put up with that – you know, urine." He jabs his pipe into his mouth again and mumbles: "Yoor-i-nation."

It seems as if everybody has spoken who is going to speak – there are so few of us who count. But now Evans, who has been fidgeting beside me, suddenly says: "Charlie don't smell." He's sitting very upright, even his maimed shoulder straightened a little. He's got bigger.

"I'm sure you can be responsible for yourself, can't you Mr Sheldon?" the psychiatrist says. "You can cope, now that it's been pointed out." But he isn't sure at all, of course, he's scribbling notes to the charge nurses on his memo pad.

Sheldon at last looks up. "It's only after ten o'clock medication . . . I feel . . . funny. . . ."

But I've noticed Sheldon trying to undress at night. He takes off his jacket and hangs it delicately over the back of his

128

bedside chair; then he starts to unbutton his shirt or unfasten his belt. But as he does so his lips tremble and his face turns white. This isn't prudishness; he's not looking round at anybody yet. But some internal panic is gripping him. The palms of his hands go smoothing over his shrunken chest and thighs, as if he's trying to save them from falling off him. Then he peers round to see if anybody's watching, and slithers fully dressed under the bedclothes.

Evans volunteers: "I'll help him undress, doctor." You could swear his shoulder has straightened out altogether.

The psychiatrist says: "Splendid. You're getting to bed later now, are you?"

Evans says quickly: "Yes, yes. I'm much better now."

The psychiatrist is still jotting hieroglyphics on his pad. He's new on the ward, but he knows perfectly well that Evans is exhausted and flat out by eight o'clock.

The moment the meeting dissolves, everybody starts clicking back into focus. The Boss grows visibly a foot bigger, while Evans and Sheldon diminish. Orgill of course stays the same, and goes off with his arm still round Sheldon, saying "If you smell, Charlie, then whadya think Prick does? I vote him the shit-heap of the year, man. . . ."

Gregory and I were never any height anyway, so we just remain as we were, transfixed at the end of the table while the Boss pins Evans: "What was all that blather about, you ikey little bastard? So Sheldon doesn't smell, huh? He fucking *stinks*! You could smell 'im back in *Bristol*."

Every second the Boss is growing huger, mounding himself up and burgeoning over the table, while Evans twitches and jumps like a rabbit until his shoulder starts creeping up on him, wrenching itself higher against his neck, up, up. He can't move away, and Orgill isn't there. The Boss says: "So we're going to undress Sheldon, are we? If you think the shrink doesn't see through *that* you're an arsehole." He rattles his knuckles underneath the table. "Don't y'know what they've got under here, Evans? They've got lie-detectors. They can tell the moment you cog the dice." He stops, but Evans can't utter. "So we're 'much better now', are we? Or is it just that we can't face the truth, like all your mob?" He cracks out his pipe-ash onto the table. "I suppose we've decided to play the good boy? We want to get out. What you going to tell 'em then, Evans? Going to pretend you don't hear the voices any more?" Evans's breath comes out in whimpers, and his shoulder is jarring somewhere at his ear. "But we know better, don't we? Two nights ago you were answering back your mummy like a kid of three."

"Evans is better, he'd be better if you just left him alone." The voice is my own. I hadn't meant it to be there, it just came. Perhaps it's the beating and drumming in my stomach which sent it up. And now Gregory's fear is jangling beside me.

The Boss turns his stare on me. He has these bulging globes of flesh instead of cheeks and chin, and his eyes are obliterated. "Since when did you recognise talking to yourself, Pashley?" His pipe starts that infernal rapping on the table. "Did you know you jabber under your breath?"

I say: "No." I don't think I jabber. I'm sure I don't. I don't know. I hear my voice dwindling: "And there aren't any lie-detectors, I'm sure there aren't. . . ."

Suddenly Evans gets up and goes, as if a spring released him, and we are left alone, the Boss and I, with Gregory beside me and the paintings staring and gnashing on the walls.

"So we don't jabber?" He's gigantic now, filling the room. *Rap-rap-rap.* "I tell you you're a fucking one-man chat-show, Prof."

I can't look into the holes where his eyes should be. My stomach is pounding up all the cold air into the top of my chest, I can't breathe hardly. He goes on: "And I'll tell you another thing, Prof., what makes it worse. We haven't been taking our drugs properly, have we? Thought nobody'd noticed, did we?" *Rap-rap-rap.* "But I've seen you make those swallowing motions – then up come the pills into your hand after the nurse has gone."

"No . . ." But I can't help it. If I take those pills they slow me up, I'm just doped, then I can't find her at all.

"No wonder you're getting so freaky, Pashley. Been giving

pills to Sheldon, have you? He's so sodding terrified he'd swallow more of anything. . . ."

But I won't stay, I slither from my seat away from him, away from that tom-tom, out into the corridor where I can't be seen, and where I might find her. Gregory goes away somewhere else, as if the Boss's anger diseased me. But I don't mind. It's better alone.

I wait to see what's he's done to me, down inside. My stomach's like a cave, its walls pushing outward, the drum beating inside it. In a minute I'll be nothing but hollowness. My legs feel suddenly light. I look at them to make sure they're there, they seem a long way down. But I hear my feet scuffing the tiled floor as I walk. So it's all right.

The corridors are filled with women coming back from somewhere, but they're all old – a shuffling snowdrift. Perhaps I'll see her. But my touring of the communal rooms has become just a ritual. She's never there. The rooms seem unable to contain her, as if she didn't know or couldn't inhabit them, as if the air were wrong.

I sit in the community hall and sip tea and try to compose myself. Luckily there's nobody here I know. I thrust my hands into my lap in case they should start to shake like Sheldon's. But they're calm, and it's all right. I just need a few minutes' peace. It's true I've been spitting back my pills. That's easy enough. You just flick them behind your teeth and make sure your Adam's apple moves in a display swallow. The nurses don't watch me much. But how can I ever find her if I'm half doped? In any case, medication can't cure my disorder. I've had just about everything over the years – tranquillisers, stimulants, injections of amphetamine, electro-convulsive, every drug going. It just proves they haven't a clue.

I walk my route to the social room more like a pilgrim now, with a pilgrim's hope of miracle. It's full of Chronics, many of them women, and the vague, broken murmur of their conversation soothes me. I stand for a moment behind a rank of wheelchairs, looking over the white heads like so many snow-hummocks, and wonder if this is how she will end.

131

Then I see her. She's sitting in the corner fingering a cup of orange juice, and opposite her a dwarf woman with chopped-off hair is gabbling on and on with tiny lurches of a deformed jaw. Sophia is looking at her with that strange, vivid intensity which I loved. But I know the blue eyes are not seeing anything much, and the other woman's gabble can't be decoded. They simply sit opposite one another in solitude, the one talking to nobody, the other listening to nothing. She's wearing a dark blue dress which she would have once derided, and has caught back her hair in a ribbon behind. She looks more institutionalised. And now the dwarf gets up and hobbles away, and Sophia goes on gazing at the place where she was, gazing with her panther-like intensity at nothing at all. That's what's so hard to bear – that the old habits of face should return, but without meaning.

But she's not in pain, I know. She's just a walking carcass. She's gone. In essence, she's dead. Yet I go and sit in the dwarf's place to bathe in her stare. Although the eyes are not the same. They're not Sophia's eyes at all. Some quality is quite gone from them. They seem to operate alone. She says: "Hullo, Daniel." And suddenly I'm leaning forward with this old fury to will her back. I ask her if she's happy and what she does all day in that ward, what she's feeling, what she's thinking, and at the end of it all she smiles distantly and says "Yes", which means nothing.

But I can't accept, I have to go on. I go on looking at the carcass of her, pretending it's all right. I pursue my old idea that she can write but not speak (this occasionally happens) and I blather on about the essay. Will she write it for me?

"Oh yes," she says.

I position myself in her eyes' unearthly focus. "*Please.*"

She says: "I'll send it to you." She looks at her watch. "I have to go."

"Why?"

"Nine o'clock. Medication."

I ask: "What drugs do you take?" Perhaps I'll recognise the kind, I think, and find some clue to her illness.

"White," she says. But they're nearly all white; and I

probably wouldn't recognise the name anyway. They use thirty different drugs regularly now, it's not like when I first came.

"What do the pills do to you?"

She stares down at her hands and slowly turns them over. "They give me rest."

"Rest?"

"Yes. Rest."

We're silent. I look at her bent head, and all at once I feel guilty.

She says: "Have you been here?"

"Have I been here long?"

"Yes."

Have I? *I can't even remember how long.* Perhaps I've been here always. Ever since boyhood. I don't know. "I don't know."

She gets up. I follow her to the door and we walk down the corridor together. I manage to stop her near an alcove, where there's a radiator and a chair. I motion her to the chair, but she goes on standing. She looks small, smaller than she did. I say: "Sophia, will you tell me your married name?"

She mumbles: "Glass . . . glass . . . now you see me. . . ."

Stop it, stop it. I'm suddenly demanding: "Tell me, did you marry Charles Stainton? Are you Sophia Stainton? Mrs Stainton?"

Her hands quiver to her face. She peeps through their fingers like a child. "Do you? Do you still see me?"

I lean against the wall and she takes the opportunity to slip past me back into the corridor. I half shout at her: "*Are you married?*"

She turns and blazes: "No!" as if I'd struck her.

Then she's going away, and I'm running after her maddened, ridiculous, my legs not working properly. Everything's just as it's always been. She's going away. Twisting on her heel, looking away from me, changing direction, never really seeing, just turning her back, leaving. I follow her. Of course she knows perfectly well what she's doing. It's all calculated. Sometimes I think she's *absolutely sane*. I don't know what she is. I catch her up and she's not looking at me, as usual, as if I don't exist. I reach out and grasp her arm. She stops.

Then, I don't know why – it may be the softness of her flesh through the dress, or her closeness to me alone there – but I find my other hand lifting to her cheek and my face moving towards hers. Her back is flat against the tiled wall. I can't help myself. I suppose you can never separate the long-loved from the past, and it seems to me that just before I kiss her some other face slips between ours, a face grown out of her own, I think, but different, gone. Then her cracked lips are recoiling from mine and I'm trying to force my tongue between them and she's wrenching her head aside. I feel the blow of her wrists hard on my shoulders. She writhes away from me. For a moment she's looking at me with pure hate. It's the only time her eyes have expression. They're hot and startled. Then she's going away.

And I haven't the strength to follow her.

Something's going wrong with my body, and I don't know what it is. During my evening shower I watched it as if it were somebody else's. It seemed to have grown much older, and I felt a remote pity for it. I wasn't even certain it was mine, or perhaps anybody's. It's just there beneath me. My nerves are pulling inwards out of my feet and hands, so that I can't understand why they're still obeying me. Perhaps in a minute they won't. The water pouring over me was hard and hot on my shoulders, but beyond my hips it diffused over somewhere unfeeling and trickled away from feet as detached as the tiled floor. I know this is only a delusion, and that when I move these feet will follow me. But each morning I can't be sure how I'm going to wake up. It's as if I'm disintegrating. Even my face: I have to keep reclaiming it in the mirror. If I don't examine it like this, it may grow away from me. I know this is only a feeling. But all the same.

In bed everything's better. Then my limbs have nothing to do anyway. I can lie there just inside the trunk of me, and it's all right. Sleep used simply to happen to me, but now I lie waiting and hoping for it. Then she comes, of course, and I close my mind against her if I can. I've had unthinkable nightmares and dreams, which have come after all this time with a terrible wildness, because normally the drugs suppress sex.

Two nights ago something' woke me. I must have been sound asleep, because I sat up to see the moonlight bright in the dormitory windows, and the shadow of their bars solid black against the curtains. Gregory whispered from the bed beside mine: "It's Sheldon, Daniel. He's crying. He's been crying for hours."

I stared at Sheldon's shape across the aisle between the beds. Moonlight filled the room. The beds looked like so many iron trolleys, in which we'd been laid for wheeling away. Sheldon was weeping; but his silences seemed crueller than his sobs, which relieved him from something atrocious. I padded over to him. His bedclothes had slipped to the floor, exposing him. He lay tensed on the sheet in a foetal ball, his fists trembling at his cheeks, his eyes tight shut. I shook him softly. He just stared at me. I said: "What's happened?"

He looked at me with stricken eyes. I turned him gently on his back, and gradually his forearms eased away from his chest and his right hand began its insidious sawing. He said: "They're taking me away."

"Who? Where?"

"To the Chronics. I'm going mad. I'll be there for ever."

I felt how cold the room was. I was shivering uncontrollably. "They won't, Charlie. They won't. Who said?" I gripped his shoulders, wanting to straighten him.

"I know they will." He was staring piteously at my hands. "After what I did. They'll never let me out now. Never. I'm going mad, Daniel. I can feel it."

"After sleeping in your day-clothes?" I joked to relieve him, but my laughter came more like a cynical whisper. "You're no way mad, Charlie. You're just a bit hung up." But I was thinking: how mad is he? Is he going?

Gregory was bending over the bed. "You'll be out soon, Charlie. I dare say you'll be out before any of us."

I thrust Sheldon's sheets and blankets back round him, until

135

only his head protruded from them, white and frail as if he'd been buried alive. His hands crept to his mouth again and bunched there on pencil-thin wrists. He said: "They can't keep you always, can they? Can they? But now that I've done what I've done, now. . . ."

I glanced over to the nurse's office, where a night lamp glowed. Sheldon started to whimper. One of his hands cusped round mine: the touch of a skeleton. He said: "I should have turned it off, but I didn't. You see, I can turn it off." He gestured at his ear. Now that his sleekness of hair was ruffled, I saw a tiny grey deaf-aid locked round the lobe like a worm. "Usually I turn it off when things get bad. The Boss or one of the others. . . . Often I leave it off for hours. But then I feel this silence in my head, you see . . . and the silence gets louder and louder, and I hear myself panicking in it . . . so I switch back into the ward . . . and then I don't know which is better, and the silence and the sounds start to torture me, and I know I'm going mad. . . ."

I pressed the button by his bed and saw a red light go up on the panel in the charge nurse's office. She came over, heavy and capable. "You just take a bit of extra medicine to help you sleep, Mr Sheldon, will you? Be better then, won't it? Here you are. I'll give you your P.R.N. dose. Nothing's going to hurt you. . . ."

Gregory and I padded back to bed. Our whispered goodnights sounded shaky, and I heard him shifting and turning for a long time. I must have dozed off, because when I woke up the moonlight had gone. Then I realised that I was curled in the same position as Sheldon had been, and that I was trembling.

"Shall we have our talk now, Mr Pashley?"

He sits in a chair opposite mine, with that pretence of equality which is foolishly reassuring even in psychiatrists. His Humpty Dumpty expression is helped along by a boyish haircut around the middle-aged face, so that he seems to belong to no particular generation and to have no particular qualities.

136

But the hieroglyphs on his notepad suggest he has things in mind.

"You may have felt yourself slowing down recently," he says. "But that's only because you could be approaching one of your bad times, so your drug dose has been a little increased. It'll be back to normal in four or five days." He smiles with his wry bud of a mouth and leafs through some papers divided by iron clips, which clink together under his fingers. I imagine him trying to decipher and collate the findings of my past psychiatrists. I feel a bit sorry for him, and no confidence at all. He looks at me with his quite pleasant brown eyes and says: "Last time we discussed the tensions in the ward, I remember, but since the next few days may be rather anxious ones for you, I think it would help to talk more personally." He lays aside the papers. "So tell me what you're finding particularly bothersome."

He makes it sound like mosquitoes. But over the past two days my hopes have been gathering around him, and I can't retreat now. I need his help – I think I equate his facelessness with power. I begin: "There's been a rather terrible coincidence, doctor . . ." And suddenly I'm telling him about Sophia. It's the only way. It may even be my last chance: a man I scarcely know. Tentatively at first, then faster, fuller, I'm coughing up all the misery and strangeness of it. There's nobody else to tell. His very impersonality makes it easier; it's a bit like praying. I even find I'm expressing belief in her sanity, then I catch myself in before he thinks I'm hysterical, and instead I give her symptoms as if she might only be an Acute suffering from a personality disorder. "I know she's not your patient, doctor, so it's hard for you to intervene. But this must be a unique case . . . and my sanity's bound up with hers. Can you look into it? Please can you . . . ?"

All this time he's been sitting there looking sympathetic and writing things down, but I suppose I should have known better than to hope for a human reaction. Even before he answers I realise he's just been attending to things in his own skull, scribbling down symptoms. Because that's all these shrinks ever do. They've created a set of structures, so they have to squeeze everything into it, like medieval monks explaining everything by divine grace and evil. They're completely self-hypnotised. And now he readjusts his glasses to his brown button eyes and says: "I think we need to look into this in greater depth, Mr Pashley. We talked once before about your feelings of loss, if you remember [I don't] in relation to women, and how this involved a fear of being abandoned."

He talks as if women were just a thing in my head. "I had a few girls before Sophia," I said, intentionally casual, "but I ditched them."

"We spoke about that too, if you remember, about self-protective isolation."

"Look, doctor" – I hear my voice approaching anger or desperation – "Can you do *anything* for this woman? I'm trying to save flesh and blood and we're just talking about abstracts."

A shadow of distress crosses his face – some sort of signal to me, I suppose, since nothing crosses his face by mistake. He takes off his glasses and polishes them with his handkerchief, frowning, then suddenly smiles as if we're going to turn over a new leaf, and says: "Mr Pashley, do you believe in ghosts?"

"No. Do you?" *Where the hell are we going now?*

"Yes, in a way I do." He's leaning towards me, his voice lowered. "You see, an upset mind finds it harder to distinguish between wish and fact. People suffer this with the dead, for instance. They wish to believe them back, and therefore they create them, and then they believe what they've created. That's what fantasies are, they're an effort to reinforce a cognitive world which is really false. We call these 'pseudo-hallucinations', he added, as if being pseudo excused them, "they're images created by the will, but still absolutely real to their perceiver." His smile had disappeared into a pucker of regret. "Now I know you can see Sophia, Mr Pashley, I realise that, but it's possible that other people can't. Perhaps she's particular to you. I'd like you to think about this, and even test it."

Sometimes you despair. How can you ever get past these fellows? And the more he disbelieves in me, the less composed and credible my behaviour becomes. I'm nearly shouting.

"You're saying I've just invented her! But all you've got to do is check out the women's wards. Why do we have to go through this charade?"

He leans forward and pats my chair-arm. He says: "We'll come back to Sophia in a moment, I promise you. But first let's approach the matter from another direction. There can be so many reasons for anxiety, you realise. Your own life, for instance, began in anxiety, when your mother left you."

Oh God, I can see what's coming. He's another Oedipal Freudian. I've had this rigmarole about my mother from so many analysts that I can reel off my answers by heart. Only today, for once, I'm angry enough to say straight out: "Look doctor, I'll save you the trouble of going on. I'm not in love with my mother, if you want to know. I loathe her. She left me when I was eight and I don't have a single happy memory of her. That's unkind, I know, since she was mad. But life is unkind."

He's unruffled, of course, they always are – like reptiles. He says a little surprisingly: "Do you ever remember her sane?"

"No. I think she behaved oddly even in my earliest memory." *Gazing at a snake in the flower bed. Her eyes look strange.*

"How old were you then?"

"I'm not sure. But I remember her hand was level with my head, so I must have been about four." Then I decided to ask him the question to which I've never had a straight answer. There's this cold shaking inside me when I ask it, but it's worth another try: "Doctor, how likely is it that I've inherited my mother's madness?" I see my hands wrenching together on my lap. I stop them. But I think of Sheldon, curled up, blinded, crying.

The psychiatrist says: "There's absolutely nothing inevitable about it, Mr Pashley. People may inherit a tendency or a weakness, but that's all."

"But are my symptoms and hers related?"

"Not necessarily, no." He glances at his papers. "She was diagnosed as paranoid psychotic. It doesn't follow that there's any relationship at all between those symptoms and yours. The truth is, Mr Pashley, that we simply know too little about these things. But your father has a record of complete stability, and no other known member of your family has suffered madness. That should reassure you. And medication is far more sophisticated now than it was when your mother was committed."

So they don't know. You just wait and see.

He asks: "Do you remember her leaving?"

And now what does he hope I'll say? That she was dragged out of the house in a strait-jacket? Well, she just went; and she didn't give a damn about her going, and nor did I. Christ. These shrinks aren't happy until they've turned your childhood into a Herodian massacre. And now the eggshell face is looking at me, hoping to get a symptom.

I say tiredly (I know this one by heart too): "Yes I remember her going. Two people came for her. Just a man and a woman in ordinary dress. I don't know who they were. I was eight. I asked them how long she'd be gone, and they said not long. My father locked himself in his room. She went quite quietly."

I watch them leave, crouched in the laurel bush by the gate. The woman says: "Poor little mite, how can you tell him she's going away for ever?"

The smell of laurel bushes still makes me sick.

"Keep calm, Mr Pashley."

"I *am* calm."

"Well then . . ."

"Look doctor, I don't see any point in this. I asked you about Sophia and we end up in my childhood. Can you please do something practical about her?"

But his fists rub at his eyes like great white grubs, and he's sighing. The shadow is over his face again. He says: "Can you not even consider that your experience of this person may be wish fulfilment, that she may be exclusive to you?"

"Wish fulfilment, doctor! There's no fulfilment about it! It's pure hell. *I don't love her anyway. I think I hate her.*" But of course it's no damn good. I know what he's going to say now: *Hate is frustrated love, Mr Pashley, don't you think that the very strength of your feelings etc etc?* Yes, I do, unfortunately. You'd think he was some kind of computer sitting there. These mind-buggers are meant to help your self-confidence, but you end up without a self to have confidence in. You're just a blob of manias and delusions. I say: "All you've got to do is check out the women's wards, doctor."

He rubs his eyes again, with that look of distress, and says: "I know the women's wards well, Mr Pashley. I was working there some months before coming here. Sophia is a very distinctive Christian name, and there's certainly nobody called that here. You must understand that the women's wards are being phased out in this hospital. Our youngest female patient is sixty-two years old."

I say in amazement: "So she's a *doctor* here!"

"There are no women doctors in this hospital."

In the silence my arms feel oddly light – I have to hold them down to stop them lifting off the chair-arms. I concentrate on this, while staring at the patch of wall behind Humpty Dumpty's head. I notice he keeps a photograph of his wife on his desk. She must be mad. He's still talking, but I can't hear it. He seems to have got farther away, so it may be the distance. But it doesn't matter. He's just one of those hospital shrinks who hold too many out-patients' clinics in their catchment area, and don't even know what's under their noses. Either that or he doesn't want to help me. It just shows how they run these places. There's an odd, high-pitched whining in my ears as well as his voice. It's no good discussing things with him. You might as well argue with a tank. He's saying how she doesn't exist, of course. You can tell by the regretful shape of his mouth. ". . . You're an intelligent man, Mr Pashley . . . can you find any sign that you might be mistaken?"

My voice, like my arms, is quite detached now. I expect it will say whatever pleases him. Perhaps it's not my voice, only his. His mouth is going up and down. I say: "I used to wonder why nobody looked at her . . ."

"When?"

"Oh, years ago." But his face clouds. "She says she's glass, you see. . . ." If you cracked his face with a spoon, I'm sure it would be egg. I think the whining in my ears is louder when I lean forward. Perhaps that's because I'm nearer him.

He's saying: ". . . Nobody of that name here. . . ."

I say: "My mother's name is Pashley still. I know she's not here. . . . She's in a mental hospital in Leeds. . . . I never said she was here."

"Of course that's absurd," he answers. "I wasn't talking about your mother. . . ."

These bloody shrinks, they just confuse you. I should have taken my drugs.

He's still mouthing things. He's looking worried. "I hope you'll check things out for yourself, Mr Pashley."

"Yes, I will. Yes of course." Better just to agree. Because in a minute I'm going to forget to hold my arms down and he'll diagnose me as a psy-something. He's farther away than ever now, isolated in his chair. But he's watching me even from there, and he doesn't look happy.

"Have you been taking your pills properly?" His eye-beams come looping over the distance.

"Yes, oh yes."

But he obviously doesn't believe me because he's still scribbling, and an hour later, when the charge nurse gives out the drugs, mine has been liquefied into a colourless syrup and I'm watched as I drink it. But the whining goes on in my ears – it's like a fault in the electricity, silvery and fragile – and my legs walk in an airy way which I'm getting to accept. I'm not even afraid of overbalancing any more, I simply rely on them to move without my knowledge. It's like treading water, except that I hear them clopping over the tiled kitchen floor or down the corridors, and feel as if somebody else is walking beside me.

And this evening, at supper time, there arrives the proof of the psychiatrist's idiocy. The nurse hands it to me in a long brown envelope and just says: "This came for you."

So she kept her word after all; and when I open the envelope in the quiet of the dormitory, eight quarto pages slide out onto my bed. Her handwriting has grown jagged and irregular, squeezed into close-lined pages, but it's hers all right. She's just scrawled above it: 'Here you are' –

Nine

Of course he's the type I always attract – Wets & Runts Inc (a doctor is a power-figure, after all). His face gazes into mine with a look of perpetuated shellshock. He reminds me of besotted medical students from my first year at college. I suppose I should feel pity, but some people's feelings are just too farcical to elicit patience, and immortal passion isn't my scene.

Daniel is always romanticising himself, as he does everything else (including, oh God, me). He has to invest his past with mystery, as if it was dense in aesthetic experience, intellectual illumination, agonised relationships etc. It's grotesquely entertaining. Because of course there's nothing in his past. Nothing. When he describes his holidays among Tuscan gardens and Sicilian temples, I know he's never been to these places – he's just leafed through illustrated books and read it all up in the library.

Cruwenath. The stagnation is almost tangible here, like mist or mildew. You long for a few days' freedom from clinical neuroses and rotting bodies. Sometimes I feel as if I only exist as something in Charles's deposit account. Do I really care? No. Because people like me are confident in their relationships. We're used to loving less than we're loved. We never have trouble keeping men, at least for as long as we want them. That's because of our ever-alluring lukewarmness.

Daniel and I: he's sunk on his haunches by my disused

143

goldfish pond. Then suddenly his fingers are clawing at my hand. His mouth has sagged open and his eyes are protruding like a cod's.

"What's this?" He lifts my finger, circled by Charles's engagement ring, an inch from my eyes.

"Oh, Daniel! I just wear this for my patients . . ." I laugh at him, wrench it off.

Why? Christ, I must be bored.

Were you really such a bitch?

I go on laughing until his lunatic gape subsides and he's even plucked up the guts to kiss me. His kissing isn't as unpleasant as I'd thought. His lips are quite soft and acceptable if you forget the fool they're attached to. When he blubbers out his love for me it isn't exactly the surprise of the week, but I begin to wonder what I'm getting into.

But it's not much. My body's a rather well-toured male province, and it's novel to have Daniel treating it as virgin. He goes crawling across it like a geologist, uncovering a stratum here, a vein there, and probing its rarer riches with a pious caution. These curious mining expeditions may take a whole evening to exhaust even the low-grade deposits of my bosom. Oh well.

I enjoy these antics in a narcissistic way. The pleasurableness of my body becomes our mutual property. I suppose he answers to some part of me which Charles doesn't touch. But I discover a quaint integrity about sleeping with him (Charles is stuffy about his rights) and his reverence makes this technical faithfulness easy. I don't think I want particularly to torment Daniel. He's tormented enough as it is. I'm just the catalyst of pain which was already waiting.

Damn you.

But there came a time when things started to change. His head always seemed to be grovelling around my stomach, performing a Freudian womb-return, and sometimes he disengaged his lips from mine with the look of that drowning rabbit. It was getting boring.

I invented a dutiful visit to a cancerous mother, and went on holiday with Charles. Charles leaves me alone in those parts of

144

me that I want undisturbed. We arranged our wedding for the winter.

A sultry day, heavy and waiting. By the time we laid out our picnic by the bridge Daniel already looked as if he was facing a firing-squad. He talked compulsively while his face grew whiter under its forelock of pubic-looking hair. I didn't even want to look at him. I just wanted him to go away of his own accord, which of course he didn't.

Why had you got my favourite food then?

I knew there'd be hell. I just hoped he wouldn't go crashing round my windows in the night or throwing himself in the river. When he at last lapsed into silence I said: "I think you need some other kind of woman. I don't know what kind. But not me."

You know perfectly well there are only two kinds – the one you love, and the rest.

His dopey expression angered me. He'd decided not to understand, he wasn't even going to try. His lower lip was trembling. He hadn't eaten a thing, of course. He never does, with me.

Then I put out my hand to him. He stared at it for a full two minutes as if it held arsenic – and when I withdrew it his expression splintered like a windscreen. I thought: I've given him his chance. His isn't love at all in any ethical sense – just need. It's the kind of mania that tries to dignify itself by words like 'devotion' and 'passion'. Absolute crap, in other words.

But you kissed me back, damn you.

A pathetic whisper: "I'll change my job. I'll just give it up."

Here we go again. "Daniel, please understand. You're only making things worse. I can't love you. I want to [I'm even lying for him] but I can't."

But his refusal to accept made everything easier. His eyes took on their irritating cod's look of bulging and dangling, and I thanked God I was getting out of all this before he went round the bend. Every common sense in him was sacrificed to this fantasy, obsession, idolatry, whatever it was.

It's only people like you who describe love like that. You only reason because you can't feel. It's not a substitute. But by God it keeps you safe.

I said: "I'm not coming back, Daniel." By now his wincing gave me pleasure. I went on with calculated slowness so that the words sank in as utterly as possible: "Understand. We won't see each other again." I added, in case he still hadn't gathered: "I'm going away for ever."

He just sat there, of course, with his look of drowning. Since he took five minutes to assimilate anything I said, I spent the interval collecting the picnic. I was damned if I was going to waste any more time here. I just folded up the tablecloth and started walking home.

His feet came thumping through the leav s behind me. We stopped on the bridge – a foot from one another, breathless. The river jittered and raved below. I could tell from his face that he hadn't accepted anything. Nothing at all. He'd just lapsed back into his infantile dreams. He was rummaging in the hamper, looking for solutions. How pathetic. He flourished the blade as if he could kill me. But of course he can't. He knows he can't. You can cut out plenty with the knife. But not that.

Not that.

Ten

All right. Yes, I know. That may not be what she actually wrote (she's probably incapable of writing at all by now) but that's what she's really like. That's the truth of her. Why shouldn't I admit it? She would write that if she could. But the mad have no voice.

I don't even know where she is. Sometimes I think she's in this ward, infecting it, leaking in through the fire-escapes and windows, or through the overhead lights at evening. It's impossible to tell. There must be a power shortage somewhere, the light is so weak. It labours over the floors and hardly reaches the walls at all. It's like an orange liquid. I think it's still dimming. The nurses go back and forth through it, disappearing into blackness on the other side, but the patients are nearly obscured.

It's closing in all the time. If Sophia's not here, then she's nearby. The air shakes slightly. If you're very still, you can feel it quivering, as though there were a heat haze. But it's cold. The Boss sits huge as a mountain now. His shoulders slope like scarps and the piggy red hairs set his hands on fire. If I have to pass him, I squirm along the wall behind his chair. That way I avoid his eye-pits. Instead I see how the back of his neck bulges into a triple crease a foot wide, and his pate is just a slab of putrefying meat. His gang mutters round him. Sometimes they swim and coalesce so close you can hardly separate them. Only in the O.T. room Prick is lifting weights the size of millstones: he just tosses them about. He knows I broke into that glass office, of course, and sooner or later he'll blackmail me. He fixes me with a dead look.

Today I found Evans blubbering in the lavatories. The Boss had caught him and scruffed at him. "So you think you're getting out of here, you fatarse?" he'd said. "I tell you, they never let *anyone* out. They just transfer you to another ward, that's all. And in the end they get you with electro-convulsive, they draw out your brain through your eye-sockets and you go up in smoke like the Jews."

Everybody knows there's a holocaust coming. Orgill's brotherhood is permanently in the dormitory now, ranged about the dead-white cubes of its beds. God knows what they do. Only at meal times they invade the Boss's dining-area, Orgill shaking his great froth of hair while his eyes half incinerate the place.

He and the Boss go preying and gorging on the rest of us. They never leave us alone. Everybody's taking sides. Only Gregory and I are in the middle, because we never could identify. You can feel the others scouring about inside our heads. They want to turn us into them. Gregory tells me: "Easy does it, Daniel, you're having one of your lows." So even he can't feel them like I can. The booming in my stomach never lets up now, and beneath my waist another person begins, I don't know who. It makes walking very peaceful, of course, I don't even have to try. I just find myself moving where I want to go.

But the staff either can't see what's coming or they take no notice. They despise us. I think they all hate us. We're useless. They can't even envisage our wounds, let alone heal them.

Just now I noticed the charge nurse beckoning one of the younger sisters into his office. I thought they were bound to be discussing the coming conflict, and I edged into hearing distance. But no. They seemed to think everything was fine. They're just abandoning us.

"You shouldn't have much trouble this week," he says. "The only one to watch is McQuitty, the one they call the Boss. He can be a bit heavy on some of the others." But that was all he thought. "And you'll find Pashley worse. He'll peak in a day or two, then lift out pretty quick. Just make sure he takes his syrup. His language deteriorates . . ."

"Oh, I'm used to that," says the nurse. She laughs.

They're still giving me my drug as a syrup, to make Sophia invisible. The nurse watches while I drink it. So I have to slink into the wash-rooms soon afterwards and get my tooth-brush. Then I tickle my throat until the syrup sicks itself up again. Sometimes this takes as long as half an hour. But I don't stop until it's all out. They're not destroying her like that.

Yet it's been five days since I spoke to her. She's evading me again. Either she stays locked up behind the iron door or else she's close, but in some place I can't reach her. This evening, at the church service, I know she was there. This quaking was in the whole building. I was near the nave's centre and I could feel her moving in the shadow of the chancel. I even heard her singing.

But I never glimpsed her. I suppose they're saving electricity even in the church, because you could hardly see from one end to the other. Above the altar, where the stained-glass Christ hung, the window was a dead, black jig-saw. Perhaps even He was no longer there. And the sound seemed to have been turned down. The priest's bawling was farther away, and whenever he stopped the mewling of the Chronics was barely audible.

By the end of the service she'd gone, of course, and I went out alone into the night. I walked across the grass and through the dark trees towards the outer wall. I couldn't feel my feet, but heard them shushing across the sward. In the old days the wall used to be floodlit, but not any more. A three-quarter moon rotted in the sky. The only other light came from the upper windows of the hospital, shining above the oaks. But they were far away. The moon threw the wall into shadow. Along its summit the broken glass wound out of sight in a snake of glinting spikes.

I smoothed my palms over the wall's surface. The network of cement between the bricks shone white and regular. It didn't offer a toe-hold anywhere, and its top loomed a full three feet above my upstretched hand. I found a sharp stone and gouged out a patch of cement, but the gap between each brick was so thin that it scarcely afforded a fingerhold, and I couldn't have levered myself off the ground for more than a second, let alone her. I walked slowly along the perimeter in the shadow, hoping for a lesion in the brick. I was quite alone. Only a cat crouched on the sharpened wall, then whispered away down the far side. Soon I had walked nearly half way round, but there was no fracture in the surface. I scanned the top for a blunt wedge of glass which might hold a looped rope. But it was absolutely regular. The fragments were sprinkled frail and sharp all along the surface, like a litter of vitreous bones.

Then I reached the drive. It coiled palely between its rhododendrons. In the shadow of the shrubbery I pushed forward until I could see the iron gates. They stood ajar. I couldn't discern the face of the porter in the kiosk; he seemed to be leaning back on his chair. My legs went through the undergrowth oblivious of me; they made no noise. I settled among the last bushes and stared. It was the elderly porter on night duty. Even when a car's headlights swung against the iron from outside, he took a full minute to emerge and ease the gates farther open. He'd probably been asleep.

I listened in silence. Then I went forward on all fours, studying my legs to see what they would do. But they were perfectly co-ordinated. Only my feet and hands made a soft crunching on the gravel. I lumbered forward like a dog. The porter didn't move. The light from his kiosk shed a long, dim parallelogram over the drive, but when I entered it his vision was cut off by the window-ledge. I passed within four feet of him, and out between the iron gates. Against the wall, and all along the far side of the road, grew thick, concealing bushes. I crouched in them while a car passed. Then I crept back beneath the kiosk and up the drive, cutting across through the rhododendrons, over the lawns to the side entrance.

By ten o'clock I was climbing into bed, while Gregory watched me from his pillow, hesitant and concerned. He said: "Are you all right, Daniel?"

"Yes, I'm all right."

I listened while the pounding in my stomach slowed to a soft, reverberant throb, grew gradually fainter in the silence, until only the silvery, unseen wires rose and tingled inside my eardrums. I closed my eyes. All she and I had to do was to listen out for cars, then move silently together over the gravel. It should be easy.

Morning medication is the worst. It takes longer and longer to sick it up, as if my throat's losing its feeling. The lavatory doors swing lockless on their hinges, so there's no privacy, and the others barge in and out. Several of the frailer ones sit there for twenty minutes at a time, unable to pass anything, and the charge nurse is always looking in. He's suspicious now.

This morning I retched for nearly an hour before I did it. My ears were ringing. Afterwards I had to lean my head above the basin, bending double over it in case my legs gave way without warning. That's how Orgill found me.

"Hey, you all right, Danny-boy?"

He came and stared into the basin. It's plughole was clotted with the remains of my breakfast, and the poisonous drug curled in a transparent smear over one side. He was burning and agitating against my elbow. I didn't want to look at him. His arm came across my back like a brand. "You must be real bad. I'll go get help. Say, fellows . . ."

"No, no."

He turns back at the door. I look up to meet his gaze flashing and bumping about my head. He opens his pink baby's hands to me, and his candour is ghastly. I think he can see everything. "You need help, man."

"I'm okay. I'm often sick." I wipe my mouth and turn on the taps. The vomit and poison swirl and merge together. "The doctor knows about it."

He's trying to get me to look at him, I know, but I concentrate on the basin while it empties. He won't keep still or go away. Now his fingers are plucking at my shoulder. "Why not

151

get doing something, Danny, instead of just moping about? Why not help us paint the dorm?"

But I can't answer.

Then the door opens. I hear Gregory's voice, and next moment his wafery hands arrive on the basin's edge. I straighten up. Orgill is jittering from one foot to the other, opening and closing his fists as if he wants to hit somebody. I say: "I'm just having one of my bad times, Orgill. I get them sometimes. It isn't anything."

But his eyes are searing between Gregory and me. "Look, you fellows, why don't you join the group? Unbutton a bit. Y'know what we need in this place?" The sunflower head is dancing and coruscating. "Hope! Light!"

Gregory coughs and squirms. He says: "We're not great joiners . . ."

But Orgill is inexorable. I can't look at him. I just hear his feet tapping on the tiles. His back is against the door and there's no other way to leave. He says: "C'mon, fellows, join the gang!" I only escape him by not really being here. I'm weightless, floating. A lot of me is somewhere else. But his voice seeps around my head. It gets in because it's gentle. And of course he knows perfectly well what I was doing.

Then Gregory says: "I'll take Daniel out. He ought to lie down."

It's extraordinary how he walks through the door and Orgill just stands aside. I follow in his steps, where he must have cleared a path, and we're going across the television room. The Boss is turned away from me, but I can hear his eyes swivelling inside their sockets as I pass. He knows about it too.

Then we're in the dormitory, and there's no one else. Just this chirping and bleeping, which I think is swallows outside but which might be in my head. I stare at Gregory to make sure it's him, and it is. On its creased stalk of neck the head is fluffed with white hair like dandelion seeds. His thick-lensed spectacles come peering into my face. "You ought to rest," he says.

I stretch out on my bed and he sits on his. His face wavers about me. Its cheeks are scooped in plaster. I say: "Thanks for getting me out of there."

152

"What were you doing?" He sounds sad, perhaps frightened because I'm leaving him.

I stare at the ceiling. It's easier to talk like that. "I was sicking up my syrup, Gregory. You see, they're trying to incapacitate me. They don't want me to find her."

He sighs and looks down. "So it's her again."

"Yes." My breathing is growing harsher. And I'm floating. The bed is just draped under me like a cloud. "I shouldn't have told the shrink about her. He wants to eliminate her. She's not in his ward."

Gregory's fingers are touched to the corners of his eyes, as if he were drawing away tears. "Oh, Daniel, I thought you were getting better." His hands go back between his knees to writhe together, then he clamps them quiet. He says almost to himself: "I wonder how long we can go on like this? Up and down . . . first me, then you . . . on and on." He taps at my arm with his fingertips, as if knocking on a door. "We've seen each other through so many breakdowns, Daniel. Won't you just listen to me this time? Listen to me."

But it's so dark in here. I prop myself on my elbows. "Will you turn on the light?"

"But it's daytime."

"Please."

He turns it on and it makes no difference. He looks frightened. The daylight just sits in the windows. It's sticky. It doesn't move. You can hardly see anything. But perhaps the darkness is suited to Gregory, to his translucence. Sunlight would only scorch through him and out the other side. I remember that I want to say goodbye to him. But I don't know how. He's such an old friend. I sit up to face him. "I want you to promise me something." I take his hands – they're dry as bunches of twigs, and he's agitating at the end of them. "Promise me you'll get out of here. I can tell you how. Just promise me. Everything's so much worse now. There's going to be something terrible."

He's trembling so much that I let him go. He says: "But it can't be that bad, Daniel, can it . . . not as bad as that? I don't think so . . ."

"But you nearly always feel it. Can't you feel it now?" I lie on the bed again and stare back at the ceiling. It's fretted with tiny cracks under the dormitories of Disturbed. I say gently: "You see, I won't be here with you. I'm leaving. I'm leaving with Sophia. I've never really told you about her, have I?"

"Oh yes, Daniel. You've often told me . . ."

"She had to leave me once, Gregory, but she's back now. We're going away together."

"Yes, Daniel. You have told me . . . I do know. But listen." He keeps adjusting his glasses to clarify not just his vision but everything, trying to see in this twilight. "You and I, we've been here such a long time. So very long . . ."

What is he trying to say? How long have I been here? I don't know. Perhaps longer than I remember. Perhaps since boyhood. I don't know. Oh God. I don't know.

Gregory shakes his head. His hand comes knocking and tapping at my arm again. "Just keep calm for a day or two longer, and you'll be all right." The distress whines in his voice.

The light is so dim now. Poor Gregory. Perhaps he's going soft in the head. No wonder. You can't read or even think here. The lamp is just a phosphorous blob.

I say: "I came here from the sheltered accommodation people."

Gregory's face is all splintered and breaking. "But we've been in and out of those for years. . . ." Then he's looking up at somebody, and I see the charge nurse walking in the darkness. Gregory calls out. "Henry, come and tell us how long Daniel's been in Faraday."

"You ought to know!"

"You tell him though." Gregory's voice is pleading. "He's getting muddled. He keeps getting muddled."

The nurse stoops by my bed and pats my cheek. "Cheer up! You're one of our *old* boys. You're one of our favourites. Nothing to be glum about."

Talk of fucking condescension. And all the time my stomach gasping and the bed just mist under me.

I get up and leave them. I don't want to hear them say how

long I've been here. Gregory lopes after me until I swear at him. I shouldn't have done it, and I must remember to say goodbye. I can't leave him like that.

Then I find a pen and write her a message, very clear and short. Just a time and a place of meeting. I know she can reach the place even late at night, because that's where the fire-escape comes down from the women's wards. I take the message to the iron door. I have to knock on the curtained panel for ten minutes before a nurse opens it. Then at last I thrust the letter into her hands, the name written huge on its envelope, and walk away quickly before she can think up an excuse for not delivering it.

The moon is standing in the windows again. All so quiet now. You wouldn't know this thing is going to happen. The patients lie asleep, even Gregory and Sheldon, mounded beneath their sheets like corpses buried under snow. And now that it's so silent, only the silvery cymbals clash far away against my ears, although the churning in my belly starts up softly as I drop my feet to the floor. How strange that it's my last night here. I go to the window and peer through the curtains and out between the bars. Beyond the perimeter wall, which moves in a black splinter under the shadowing moon, the lights of a village flicker, and above them the valley lifts into the hills – the hills of our freedom, rolling like bones under the blanched sky.

Up in Disturbed, someone is weeping.

Eleven

I must keep calm and not be noticed. I'll go wherever the others aren't. Stay very still, to stop the airiness altering or creeping up. Let everything inside me wait, so I can use it when I have to.

The ward is quiet, because the Boss is with the kitchen porters. There's scarcely any light. Sometimes they switch it off inside the window-panes. Then an inky lava crawls along the walls and rustles out from under the chairs, where it's been waiting. Outside, the park and the hills turn opaque. You can hardly see them. The lava laps at the sills and coagulates in pools wherever you look.

I'm not taking any chances. This morning I spew up the poison under the shower, and it comes quite easily. Below my ribs the water drips off glint by glint, and I hear it clashing on the tiles. When I move I still can't feel the floor, but my thighs are full of the reverberation of my walking, and it's all right. I watch while the poison writhes away down the plug; it doesn't come back.

I go into Industrial Therapy, because the others are in Occupational. I keep my eyes down. But the thunder in my stomach shakes in my hands, so I have to hold very still. We're packing microscope slides into sanitised packets, and they slither under my fingers. Sometimes they're nearer than I think and my hands go splashing and sparkling among them, like in waterfalls. But nobody notices. I just try to stop the air from

156

expanding in me somehow, keep very quiet and don't talk to a soul. The minute-hand on the wall edges to one o'clock.

We're meeting at nine this evening and I can't put off my packing much longer. Not that there's much, but I have to be sure. When I look into O.T. it's nearly empty, but Gregory is building up a new sculptured head. He dabs and smudges squeamishly at it. The woman's portrait has gone, and he's shaping a man's now. I remember that I must say goodbye to him. But I must keep this breath quiet inside me. It's as if my skin were brittle, and noise may gash it. I walk delicately round him. "How's it going?"

"Oh, it's hard to tell just now." It's a sad head, like all Gregory's, with a loose mouth and long, scored cheeks. He says: "Don't you recognise it?"

"No." I don't think it's much good. He can't do hair. And the eyes are odd, overcast.

He goes on shaping the long nose, smiling to himself.

I say: "I'll leave you to it." I'm glad of his preoccupation.

Just outside Faraday I look through the windows to make sure the iron gates are still there at the end of the drive. From here the air is whiter; I can even glimpse the porter's lodge. The lawns look sodden and green, and in the old football-grounds of the Acutes the rotting goalposts rise from a lake of daffodils. Somewhere beyond, there's a shimmer of water.

But the moment I enter the ward the air is jangling and crying, and it's too late to go back. I'm pinned to the wall. The room's centre vibrates with a lacework of wires and criss-crossing beams. So I can't move. Something rubs against my elbow and I see Evans nailed there like me.

"What's happened?"

"It's the Boss," he whispers. "Somebody took his money. He says."

The Boss is heaped on his chair in the middle of the room, the only place there's light. He's so huge that his head brushes the ceiling and his child's mouth is tensed open under the stone circles of his cheeks. From time to time he smacks the back of the neighbouring chair with the palm of his hand, or digs his fists into the pockets of his coat lying on it. Then he wrenches the pockets inside out and his head jerks up again to see if anyone has moved. But nobody has. The grey-red locks seethe round his face. "Who did it? Who did it?"

But they are all seated immured in the darkness, or suffocated against the wall like us. Gregory has arrived too, and stays flat against the doorway. I can only see the orbs of his spectacles. But the Boss can see everything. His pipe starts its atrocious beating on the arm of the chair. His eyes drill and stab along the seats. The tarry blackness is coiling everywhere now, but he sees right through it. His head turns ninety degrees and impales Sheldon in his chair. His pate looks putrescent, it's starting to stink. He says: "Mr Sheldon, you haven't by any chance . . . ?"

Sheldon can only whisk at his violin, he can't answer at all.

Then the Boss's eyes are back machine-gunning the walls. They leave circles of ash wherever they hit. The only sound is voices squeaking on the television screen. And the tremendous rapping. He says: "Mr Nisbet, you're not aware of having any extra money with you?"

Gregory twitches and jumps against the door. "No . . . no, I haven't . . . no . . ."

The Boss's eyes are grinding and jabbing round the walls towards me. I can feel them coming, and I can't move. I try to press back into the wall's dark, but it's no good. And now they're here and I'm still spiked to the wall. "Perhaps we remember seeing something, do we, Mr Pashley?" *Rap-rap-rap*. "I'd be grateful if we can remember."

Somebody else's voice, flittering and tiny, speaks out of me. "No, I don't remember."

But his stare pushes hard against my chest and I can't breathe. He says: "We didn't happen even . . ." *rap-rap-rap* ". . . to pick anything up off the floor?"

"Nothing."

I only know his eyes have gone away when the spikes lift out. I still don't move. The clock says ten past four but it's pitch dark. Just glints and spurts of dimness where the Boss is.

Then suddenly Tom Orgill is laughing in the doorway, beating his enormous, tender fists together. "Hi, fellows!

Anything good on the telly?" As he strides across the room he disconnects all the criss-crossing wires. They just go dragging and trailing at his feet and he doesn't even notice, while great ingots of black light melt in the corners. People are suddenly shifting about. Then Orgill stands in front of the Boss, and new ingots clank into place between them. "Say, Boss, what's the worry? You got the clap?"

"Don't twit me, Orgill. One of you gone and filched fifty-five quid out my coat, and I wanta know who."

The blackness is oozing up out of the floor cracks. Everybody's stopped moving again.

Orgill spreads his great hands. "Search me, Boss. But it won't be one of my boys. We're not into money."

"Don't give me that hyper-glanded bullshit, Orgill. Just tell me if you've seen anything?"

"I?" Orgill sticks a pink thumb in his own chest.

"*You.*"

The black lava is frightful now. It's lapping at the skirting and heaped in scuds along the ceiling. I start to worm along the wall towards the dining-area.

"Are you accusing *me?*" Orgill is suddenly seething. His face has turned pinker. He's trying to incinerate the Boss.

But the Boss's eyes are already burnt out. "I'm not *accusing* anyone."

The next moment Orgill is saying: "Let's get away from here, boys! This room kinda stinks!" And seven of them troop into the dormitory.

But nothing returns to where it was. Everything pulses and judders. Even the furniture is swaying in the overloaded air, and the vases and pictures only stop their seesaw when you stare hard at them. I sit down. This thrumming rocks my body. The last light in the room is being choked by cigarette smoke. The patients just stay where they were, gazing up at the scuffed rectangle of the television hanging in nothing.

If only I knew where she was. The clock says quarter past four – there's plenty of time – but now the Boss and his gang have gone to play poker in the dining-area and Orgill's clique are in the dormitory. So I can't gather my clothes: I just have to

159

wait. And hope this thing won't break. Because everything's waiting for it. Even outside, the trees have gone still and there's nobody walking anywhere. It's like a painting. The clock is slowing down. This juddering in the room too – it's waiting. And when it breaks I don't know how far it will spread.

But not to her. She and I will be gone. Out there in the dark, there'll only be us. She'll have to entrust herself. Then it'll be over at last. Sophia, don't not be there. You can't not be there. I'm coming. I just need to get my things. We'll go soon. We'll go back.

This frailty in my body has continued a long time. It's good it's so dark, otherwise they'd see me. There's a nurse sitting with us now. But he doesn't alter the blackness much, only sits in his own patch of white. I concentrate on the people in the television: she's watching them too. And it's six o'clock.

They ought to leave the dormitory for high tea now, but they only come out two at a time. I sit alone in the dining-area. I don't know when I'll get another meal. But by the time Orgill emerges, his followers are back inside. He eats fast, famished. Five minutes later he's gone again, and it's after seven. And nothing's got better. The lights are on all through the ward, but they just hang there in their own blackness. I don't know what to do.

Very gently I get up and peer through the panel into the dormitory. It's ashen white. The marble beds extend forever. Around the most distant one, they're sitting with their arms outstretched. There are others with them now, elderly ones, white-haired or white-bearded. They don't seem to move.

There's nothing else for it but to squeeze open the door. It's soundless, and none of them look at me. But the sitar music fills the room with its terrible shimmering. It's like those silver threads being plucked in my eardrums. You realise it has been going on always – summer air whining with insects, forever. Only sometimes it vibrates a little louder, like a faint, atmospheric intensification. And Buddha is reading his texts in a high, tense voice. And Orgill's eyes are scorching them all with that soft, unbearable fire, preparing them for battle, while his great flaxen head goes nodding from one to another.

I keep my eyes on the floor, and move towards my bed. I crawl under it, and my wardrobe door eases open on the far side. I'll take the big haversack. I don't know how strongly I can walk. Or she. But we shouldn't need much. I lift the clothes out noiselessly, under the level of the beds so nobody can see. Underwear, washing things, scarf. My whole body is numb. I take a spare pullover for her, and fold my raincoat in a tight wad. I can't find my torch (the Boss's gang steal) or any handkerchiefs. I slide off my soft shoes and start lacing on a heavier pair.

Now the mosquito whining of the sitar is joined by the tabla drum. It thuds and plops and taps. Then it's gone. My fingers fumble with the old-fashioned laces, while the notes of the sitar shift and vibrate again. I lace the shoes tight. Then I softly close the wardrobe doors. And suddenly the tabla is back. It's scuttling and nagging like a heart-beat, and underneath it booms another, deeper sound. But I don't know where this is. It groans in my stomach or my head. The drum patters and panics over it. I feel light. I stare over the bed, but I can't tell what they're doing. Orgill sits enormous there. His head towers and glitters in its fractured halo. They're passing fire to one another on their fingers. They're eating or sacrificing something. The sitar ripples and stretches their faces into ghastly grins, and the tabla goes pad-pad-pad-pad like soft things dropping. My legs are trembling against the floor-boards. I can't stop looking. I think I'm witnessing something unspeakable. Buddha's coat glints in an armour of badges and his hands lift his book. I shut my eyes and start crawling back under the bed. I daren't look behind. I just hear the sitar freezing their grins, and the tabla's tapping and that other deep, colossal reverberation.

When I reach the door I'm suffocating. I press it open and push into the television room. But nobody's looking. They're sucked against the images flickering in the smoke. Their mouths have fallen open. So I creep behind the chairs. I'm wading in the black lava, and it covers my bag.

But, oh God, you can't go on like this. You have to rest. And I lean back against the glass door into the dining-area, and drop the bag onto my feet where I suddenly feel it. Then I listen to the gasps of my breath until they quieten. Because I must quieten. I must. And it's easier here. This whole room is empty, embalmed. The vast, impending fission has frozen it.

Behind my back, I know, the Boss and his men are holding council in the dining-area, and I have to pass through it to the kitchen, then out. I don't know how soon to go, but it's no good waiting. I check my watch by the clock and there's hardly any time. I mustn't look through the glass first. Just go. If I carry the haversack low, by its straps, they won't see. So I open the door a foot, then edge in backwards and see the kitchen only a stride away.

But I can't stride and the moment I'm inside the Boss's voice says: "Get 'im, get 'im."

I jump and nearly drop the haversack. But they're not looking at me. They're clustered round the table – six of them now. Their black coats and hair seethe and merge, and their cards are fanned in metallic scales under their chins. I don't know what game they're playing. The Boss has his back to me, but his pate is smoking and rotting like a corpse and the eyes of all the others are on me. They hold the metal cards close against their mouths, like microphones. They mutter into them. The whole room is whispering and crackling with impatience. The Boss's head is in dusty red flames. I take a step towards the kitchen and I'm almost there. The Boss can see me, of course, but he doesn't move. And the next moment I'm through the doorway.

But I know I'm not safe. I can't afford to rest. I pick open the doors of the food cupboards, but everything jangles when I touch it. I sit down on the edge of a chair and run my hands over my legs, shoulders, arms, face. They coalesce and I can believe in them. I have to hold them together. It's quarter to nine. But it'll be all right. In here you can hardly hear anything. I scrabble through the food-shelves trying to find a picnic. We'll have to eat in the hills. Perhaps for as long as a week or two, until they forget us. I wrap things in a dish-cloth – bread, butter, marmite, a tin of sausages, sweetcorn – then tuck them into the haversack. It's not much. I kneel down and hunt through every shelf and rack, but there's only carrots and biscuits. Then I take the tin-opener and the bread-knife. And it's done.

But when I stand up again and listen, the noise is awesome. I don't know what it is. It's coming from everywhere: tingling, precipitous. I lift the bag onto my shoulder and turn to go. But I think it's starting. Because the noise is out there too. The air is breaking apart. Yes, it's beginning. I wait to see my feet moving. They tremble. I'm made of water. The voices next door are muttering. And now the whole wall is a shouted mutter, louder and louder, banking up and up against the thin partition. But I can't move. I just stand. Until it rises, swells, at last bursts and shatters the plasterboard in a terrible, hoarse staccato: *"Get 'im, get 'im, get 'im."*

I can't find the door handle. It must have fallen off. I can't get out. My fingers are pattering over it. They're miles away. It's starting and I'm too late. The noise is a tornado now. I bury my head against the door and block my ears, but it goes on in my head. It's cracking open. And another sound is piercing it, lifting above the rest with icy soullessness, the shimmering sitar, the dreadful everlastingness, and Sheldon is striking his violin and it's screaming.

Then the handle turns and I'm in the corridor. I'm trying to run. I can feel my feet. I'm still clutching the haversack. My shoes echo down the passage. It's empty and I'm alone. My watch says five to nine. I'm running down the intestines of a worm. Its walls are filmed with slime and it's flittering and gibbering with Chronics now. They're all the same age, no age at all. They jabber as I go, they whimper in the dormitories.

Sitting on a radiator, in a bend of the passage, all day, spitting on himself, he's covered in saliva. "Go away, get away. Body, stinking body, get away . . . ah! Aaaaaagh! . . . stinking corpse. . . ."

Then I'm through the side-door and the wind comes cool and peaceful on the stroke of nine. I arch back tenderly against the wall and listen to the spreading spaces and the huge sky, and there's no sound except my own panting and the barking of a dog far away in the village. Overhead a great blanched moon dangles, and smooths the garden into frost – frost on the trees and the splintered glass and the hills. I stare up behind me. The fire-escapes dribble blackly everywhere, scarring the building in pain-lines. The one which descends from the women's wards zigzags down from iron landing to landing, dark or pale in the moonlight. I walk to its foot and she's not yet there.

So I wait.

The drive still curls sickly yellow through the rhododendrons, away to the porter's lodge. I imagine the iron gates jarred quarter-open, somewhere beyond. I lay my haversack under the iron stairs, and sit on their last step, and go on staring up. The hospital rises in a Gothic card-palace. Its thousand windows glimmer in the night sky. How strange! They're cold and far as the Arctic. I'll never go back.

But as I wait the place starts to rock with what is inside it. I get up and stand away. One by one the lights are going out. As if it's dying. I watch the fire-door of the women's ward. She doesn't emerge. Somewhere in there she's turning out the lights. I wait for her. But she's so untrustworthy. You can't believe her. And suddenly I know she's not coming. That she'll never come.

She does it on purpose, of course. She's known all the time. And now I can feel the sensation in my limbs again. I've felt them all evening, I think. My feet hard and rasping on the grass. But it's not right. The numbness gone, and she not here. It's nearly ten o'clock and she's still turning out the lights. The whole building quakes and groans with its memories. I go to the base of the iron steps to pull my bag from underneath.

And somebody's there. In a maze of shadows she's gathered under the stairway, then she steps frightened into the light. She's wide-eyed. One hand pats her hair, and her tongue runs nervously round her mouth.

I can't speak. I step towards her lightly, as if she might vanish. Then I reach out and touch her hands. They're real, and a little rough. I just say: "You're late."

She says: "I'm sorry."

Her blue eyes look black and the moon has whitened out her lines so she seems young. I grasp her hand, but she draws back a little and I'm afraid to kiss her. I go on holding her fingertips. I whisper: "Have you got your things?"

She nods, and pats something white over her arm.

I can't tell if she realises why we're leaving. My thumb and forefinger circle her wrist. I draw her fractionally closer and stare hard at her to make her understand. "This whole place. It's starting to shake. Can you feel it shaking?"

"Yes."

"That's why we're leaving. You do want to leave, don't you? Tell me you want to leave." She only lifts one hand to her face. "You're coming with me now."

For an instant I relinquish her hand to gather the haversack. When I look round she's farther off, and one foot hovers on the metal stair. My stomach jolts and tears. I reach out. Her hand isn't there. She draws back another step. She looks down vacantly. "Well, it's time I went back."

"*Back?*"

Oh God, don't. My throat is filling with sickness. I can't move. I just stare up at her. She's starting to mount the steps. Her voice seems to be coming from a long way away. Her face is chalk-white in the atrocious light. "We can't go on, Daniel. I'm leaving you . . . I can't love you. I want to but I can't. You frighten me."

I open my mouth but nothing comes. She's circling the stairs without a sound, higher and higher. Her words come clear and small from far above. "I'm not coming back. I'm going away for ever. We won't see each other again." She's reached the second landing now. She's no more than a white shape against the dimness high up, climbing back, back into the black façade, the iron door which covers her. "It's not the end of the world."

"*Please, please.*"

Then my feet are drumming and crashing on the iron. They flounder and stride up three steps at a time, while my elbows jar against the railings and the haversack swings and bangs. I

165

lurch outwards and see her still climbing. She doesn't look down. My breath is coming in squeaks and my eyes are dizzy with the black-striped shadows rushing underfoot and over the walls. The ground below has dwindled away and the next moment I glimpse the whiteness of her ankles flickering on the landing just above me. She pauses and turns to face me on its bridge.

We're panting in unison, and I'm standing close to her. She's close against my hands, almost touching my chest. And suddenly the panic and the cold fanning air have gone. My breath has turned quiet. Just behind her head, glistening with its moon's hair, our hills are stricken with silver.

The haversack slips from my shoulder, leaving the knife in my hand. The river murmurs and spatters its rocks below, and it's very peaceful. Then at last, at long last, my hand is pressing up through her hot returning blood which bathes my chest, and my arm is following it deep into her body, searching, while all the life of her comes pulsing against it, and my fingers are clutching the heart which struggles and throbs, and suddenly we're falling.

Twelve

There was a jug of daffodils standing on the window-sill, and as the sun turned around it the thin stalks, slightly fibrous, changed from emerald to muddy green; and the trumpets of the flowers, frilled back a little from their stamens, were continually perforated or brightened by the wheeling light. I remember wondering what drug they had given me, that I could lie there transfixed for hours by this chiaroscuro, but I never asked.

After a long while I realised that Gregory was sitting near me with his hands delved between his knees. He had been reading a book, which was discarded on the bed beside him, and he was watching me with a mournful intentness. I had a feeling, too, that the charge nurse Henry was standing in the room, but I couldn't see him.

I had no idea how long Gregory had been sitting there, and I felt I ought to ask him something; but I didn't know what. I wondered vaguely where I was and what had happened in the battle.

He leaned towards me a little, as if I had faintly spoken. "You're in Disturbed, Daniel. What battle?"

"Nothing?"

"No."

Henry's voice said: "He's still hazy."

Gregory continued leaning towards me, adjusting his spectacles and frowning a little. I said: "Where did they find me?"

"On the fire escape."

"Being a bad boy," Henry said from somewhere out of my vision. "Trying to climb into the women's wards, were you?"

I tried to find him with my eyes, but couldn't. Instead my gaze settled back on the daffodils. Their back-lit heads were scored with tiny seams, and the hindmost petals might have been woven.

"Was I alone?"

"You don't think anybody else would join in such a fool's thing, do you?"

But all that was a long time ago. Nowadays daffodils strike me as pretty but irrelevant, although I still walk in the parklands, especially in winter, and watch the snow that comes down from the hills and falls on this asylum which is my mind.

But the inmates have mostly gone away or died now – my mother too (poor mother) – and other people have moved into the ward: a mechanic, an actor. I don't have much to do with them.

Sophia is dead too. I don't know when she died. But one day she simply wasn't there any more. That's how people go here in the asylum. You don't notice (they wheel them out very quietly, at night) and because they're very old, you're reconciled to it, they've been fading so long.

In Gregory's lucid moments, which are fewer now, he believes he must be transferred to the Chronics. I think so too. He seems to be slipping away. There won't be much left of me, then. I don't know what their final plans are for me. But life isn't exactly empty, not even here, not even now. Every morning, looking through the barred windows, I see Orgill's sun lifting over the earth, and I feel moved in a way.